Fat City Blues

by Charlie Brown

luckymojopress.com

Edited by Sue Baiman (http://myeditorissue.com)

ACKNOWLEDGEMENTS

To Podiobooks.com for hosting the initial audiobook. The lengths they have gone to help indie authors get exposure is excellent.

To all of my Metairie friends. I had to write what I know.

To all of the bars and restaurants mentioned in this book. Some are still with us, some are gone, but all made Fat City what it is and was.

PART ONE: GOLDEN BOY'S RING

A classy joint. That's what they all said about Don Quixote's. The Black Brothers tried to make a statement when they opened in 1969, that a couple of bohunks who changed their unpronounceable last names could create someplace sophisticated away from the French Quarter and establish Fat City as the true sportsman's paradise.

Just before midnight, Tony Murano closed the front door, a big oak number wreathed by wrought iron that shouted "Spanish" to drinkers finding their way into this bar. He scanned the place, noting the red tablecloths surrounded by leather-covered wood chairs and the cut glass lanterns screwed into sconces that resembled the street lights down in the Quarter.

"How the fuck do I know the word 'sconce," he asked himself, wiping his hand from forehead to chin, trying to figure out where his hosts were when they lumbered out from the back room.

"Tony, zo glud you could stop by." Zed, the older of the Black Brothers, still had an old world tongue. And even though some would think them twins, stomachs rounded over their belts like waves waiting to crash and thick salt and pepper hair curving straight back like cockscombs, two year younger Zelco slurred out the sounds of pure Jefferson Parish.

"Where y'at, kid?" He groaned, dropping into one of the chairs. "I don't move around so good no more, so we'll talk here."

Zed sunk into one of the cushions with a little more grace and motioned for Tony to sit, doing so after removing his leather jacket and draping it on the seat back before he slid into his chair.

"A drink?" Zed's voice was much deeper than his brother, like a movie vampire.

"You got Schlitz?"

"Cans and cans of it. Ve shull have some vine." Zed nodded and Zelco whistled through his fingers. Eula, Zelco's daughter, stuck her head though the kitchen door.

"Bring us da bottle, baby. And Tony wants a Schlitz."

"Sure thing, pop."

"Zo, you and your boys never come by here, Tony. Don't you like it?"

"Mr. Zed, I ain't ever sure if we're welcome."

"Don't say that, kid. We known you since you was little. You can always come in here, as long as you ain't in no trouble-causing mood."

Tony turned his eyes to the floor. "You know I ain't gonna be that guy. But, unfortunately, I'm responsible for my crew. They good boys, but they ain't always under control. This place is maybe too classy."

"Ve do encourage class, Tony. It's vhy lights are amber. The golden glow elevates any space."

Tony nodded. "Amber equals class. I'll remember that if I ever get my own joint."

The kitchen door opened and Eula walked out with a tray. She had a natural turn to her hips that would have made her the queen of any cakewalk, her forward momentum steady and flat. She swept the tray onto the table, wine glasses three-quarters full of golden liquid next to the half-empty bottle. She placed the sweating 12-ounce can on a scarlet paper napkin in front of Tony and gave him a half smile. A thousand sticks of dynamite exploded in Tony's chest.

She turned, flipping her board-straight raven hair that fell just above her belt. Tony watched it cascade into place, then turned to the brothers who held up their glasses. He raised the can and they sipped.

"She done with college?"

"Yeah. Don't know if I want her in or out da bizness. I mean da bar here, not our other bizness, of course."

"Of course. And therefore ..."

"Yeah. Zed?" Zelco looked Zed in the face.

"Yayss. Ve have a problem with Alvar." Tony knew the dwarf. He owned Que Sera, the bar across the street. The dwarf had a big mouth and nobody knew if he could back it up. There were rumors of kneecappings and hamstringings with a hunting knife, but nothing had happened in the last few years. Of course, not as many people went into his bar anymore. "His prize should have been ours."

"Really?"

"Yes, indeed. That lil' prick don't know what's good fer him. And he waves it in our face every fucking day." Zelco smacked his wine glass down, drops swooping onto the table.

"So, you were both in that game?"

"Yayss. Right there in that corner." Zed waved over his shoulder. "God's witness, kid. God's witness."

Tony looked Zed in the face. "This I gotta hear."

The game. Every regular in every Fat City bar knew about the poker game. Just like everybody says they were in Tulane Stadium when Tom Dempsey hit the 63-yard kick, everybody talks about the poker game that Alvar the dwarf won in 1970. The facts are never the same, like who else was at the table, whether Alvar had three of a kind or a flush or some kind of cockeyed straight and why in God's name it got that out of control. But there are a few indisputable facts:

1. Two of the people sitting at the table were Jim Taylor and Paul Hornung.

2. Alvar kept pushing when Hornung thought he had an unbeatable hand.

3. Hornung bet his Super Bowl ring when he ran out of cash.

4. Alvar had the better hand and won the ring.

The reason all of this was indisputable was Alvar had the ring boxed in glass and mounted on the wall at Que Sera. A framed photo of Hornung hung over it, a brass plate below commemorating the whole deal. Most people went into the place just to see it, sometimes even buying a drink. And now the Blacks said it should be theirs.

In 1970, Fat City hadn't reached its potential, but there were a few spots where a back room and an open bar could feed a poker game. Jim Taylor had played with the Saints in their first year and preferred the dark watering hole the Blacks owned to any of the glitzy burlesque clubs down in the Quarter. Besides, the hippies and their go-go shit cut into the good stuff, like Pete Fountain and Al Hirt. The fullback just wanted to drink a few drafts in peace.

Back in '67, the Saints got the bright idea for their debut season to reunite Hornung and Taylor in the backfield. Golden Boy even came to training camp, but the neck injury that kept him out of the Super Bowl forced him to quit football forever. Taylor, still the LSU boy at heart, retired to south Louisiana, starting his own business. When Super Bowl IV came to New Orleans, Hornung decided to reunite again for a weekend of drinking, basking in the nostalgia and maybe grabbing some stray tail.

It was a long way to Sunday, though, and Thursday night the former Packer backfield got invited by the Blacks to a low-stakes poker game. Most of the time the brothers set up tables and took a banker's cut, but, with such illustrious guests, they kept it small and dealt themselves in. Alvar showed up uninvited, but his case of top shelf Scotch earned him a seat.

Again, this game was low stakes. The brothers had only about 200 bucks in change as Zelco had put off the weekend bank withdrawal to make a pot of oyster stew. They told their guests forty bucks should be plenty, because this was drinks, eats, cigars and if a few cards got flipped that was a good thing.

But Alvar, he had this streak. Maybe it's because he didn't stand as tall as the table. Maybe it's because he's got a big nose, so he's ugly too. And maybe it's because the only snatch he could run down was in the cathouse owned by the Blacks, his main competition, who didn't even want him in their poker game. But he worried you, whether he thought it was right or wrong, not letting go of anything, as if his mother was a mule and he had to prove he's an ass.

The night didn't belong to Alvar. Maybe Zed and Zelco weren't trying real hard. Butchie and Todd caught a few pots, but they were more interested in stories about what a dipshit Bart Starr was. Hornung and Taylor kept talking because they had a spotlight shining on them, all the while pulling pots like hooked trout. Alvar watched his chips dwindle over two hours until he was close to 60 bucks in the hole.

He had brought a Franklin with him, which nobody noticed.

He asked for more chips and, again, nobody noticed. Then Todd called a game of Down The River, three down four up, and, as the first two came down and second two came up, Alvar pushed the pot.

He probably just wanted his money back. Who wouldn't? It's hard to lose so much, especially if you aren't some hotshot ballplayer. In the meantime, Hornung showed straight, his up cards of jack-ten-nine sitting there like a giant tongue about to release a Bronx cheer. Butchie tried to keep up with Hornung and Alvar, but, when the eight fell in front of Golden Boy, he folded quickly. But Alvar raised 20, showing king high.

"Pocket kings, friend?" The halfback's smirk razored Alvar, who's eyes narrowed.

"I'm sure you can afford to pay to see."

"Damn straight I can afford it." And Hornung moved in every chip.

Alvar couldn't match. He hopped up on his chair and pointed at the halfback. "The fuck is this? You trying to show me up?"

Hornung laughed and everyone in that room knew he was doing exactly that.

"Buddy, I just don't believe you can win. And you'll have to pay to see if I can."

Alvar turned around and punched the top of his chair. Problem was he hit it at the wrong angle and howled in pain. Hornung and Taylor fell out laughing, the rest joining them. Alvar rubbed his hand, then reached into his pocket, pulling out a key ring.

"Cadillac. 1957 convertible. Champagne. This baby is cherry. That's what I'll raise with."

"You drive a Caddy? With those legs? Bullshit." Hornung barked a laugh.

"It belonged to my brother. He died in Vietnam."

Zelco chimed in. "I seen it. Sweet ride. But c'mon, Al. You can't do this."

Zed almost put his fist through the table. "Dees was a friendly game. You don't ruin it."

Hornung was the wrong guy to taunt. He'd won the Heisman and NFL championships. Was he gonna let this little prick get over on him? No way. So, he called. He took off his Super Bowl ring, dropping it on the pile of chips.

"Show me, you little fuck." He turned over the queen, his straight legit. "Show me how you beat that."

And damn if little that son of a bitch didn't flip three fucking cowboys to join the one showing.

Hornung went batshit, flipping the table. The ring skittered away, but Alvar jumped on it like a dog chasing his favorite squeaky toy.

"You gonna welsh, Golden Boy? You want this thing back even though you lost?" Hornung ran his hands through his hair, the famous blonde now streaking gray, but Alvar didn't let up. "You'd have driven away my Caddy, right? Show me what kind of man you are."

Give the tiny bastard credit. He knew exactly what to say. Hornung paced back and forth, even drew back his fist a couple of times. But he composed himself as best he could.

Walking to the coat rack, he said, "Come on, Jim."

"Paul, you can't."

But Hornung put on his long leather coat, flipping up the collar.

"The fuck does it matter? I didn't even play in the goddamn game."

He walked out, Taylor on his heels. Alvar stared at that ring as if it had been bestowed to him by God Almighty. His smile stretched into a giggle that became a whoop of joy.

Butchie and Todd scooted on the heels of the footballers. But this was Zed and Zelco's place. And they talked softly to themselves.

Alvar sat entranced, like a kid who can't believe he got exactly what he wanted on Christmas morning. He shined the ring on his sleeve and hovered it over his finger when Zelco's shadow covered him.

"Okay, baby, get up." Zelco lowered a hand and pulled Alvar up.

"Is a thing of beauty, yays?" Zed had reset the table, somehow finding a glass of tokay wine.

Alvar looked up at Zed through Zelco's knees.

"Are you crazy? It's fucking amazing. Seriously, maybe one hundred people have one of these. And now, so do I."

Zelco screeched out a chair and sat.

"There's a little bit of irony to all this, my man. Ya see, me and Zed, we wuz talkin' to Hornung just dis afternoon about making dis here ring part of our new joint. Put in a glass case, a framed photo of him in the Heisman stance, all dat. As you can see, he ain't that attached to it."

"Yeah, that's funny. Cause that's what I was thinking about doing at my place."

"Zat leetle hole in ze wall? With the seven bar stools and no room."

Alvar waved his right finger at Zed while looking at the ring resting in his left palm. "See, it ain't gonna be like that much longer. I got plans to buy up the whole building. Make it bigger and better. I even got the name: Que Sera. What's more classy than Doris Day?"

"It don't bother us whatcha do wit' dat place. But we really want the ring. And I believe we have something you might want."

Like any dark presence, the Blacks knew how to tempt Alvar. He needed money and he needed respect. But they had something right out of his reach.

"You visit ze house three, four times a week, no? And you always go to Maria."

Alvar hadn't known how hands-on the brothers were with the brothel, but now he did. He wasn't sure he liked it. "She's very nice to me. Of course, I always pay well."

Zelco held up open palms. "Maybe you don't have to pay no more. Maybe you get proper courthouse papers. Maybe we go so far as ta throw the reception at the Lion's Hall on Hickory. Booze, food, da whole deal. And maybe then, you give us that ring. As a sign of friendship and brotherly love."

Alvar's eyes crossed, his brain slowly ripping itself in two trying to decide if this bauble was worth the woman he loved. "She could leave me right after."

"Ve couldn't allow zat. Ve have means to guarantee a long, happy life."

But as he looked at the ring, it captured a sparkle from the lamps. In that shining light, he decided a whore was a whore no matter how much you loved her. But a golden ring, this golden ring, was permanent.

Zelco saw what Alvar decided before the dwarf could open his mouth. The big man dived out of his chair, grasping at the ring while he fell.

"Gimme dat!" He flailed on the floor like a beached octopus and rolled onto his back, trying to tackle the midget. But Alvar was quick, jumping away from the meaty grasp.

"Fucking hell, you freak. Ain't no way you ever gonna touch this."

He ran out the door, flinging it back to get a satisfying slam. But Zed caught it before the desired effect. "Don't come to thees bar! Don't go to house! You never see Maria again! I see you even near me again, you dead!"

Tony looked at the two men as they looked at the floor, Zelco dragging his right foot over the carpet. Tony tried to stifle a laugh, but it bubbled out of his mouth unbidden.

"That's a bit on the overdramatic tip, ain't it?"

"Yeah, he might not have said that exactly."

"But thees I mean. Ve have not put eyes on dat son of beetch since."

"So, he's got a bar right across the street and you ain't even seen him in two fucking years?"

The Blacks couldn't meet his eyes. Tony drew himself up, figuring a point might soon be made. Zelco made it.

"We want the goddamn ring and we don't care how we get it."

"But I svore not to see him ever. And I do it for both of us."

"I believe they call that a pickle," Tony said. "But I know what to do."

"Ve can make this worth your vhile."

"I think a favor to y'all might be worth something someday, so I will expect no compensation."

"You alright, kid. We get dat ring, you'll get sumpthin'. Dat's a promise right there."

"And you just so happen to call me over on the night Que Sera is closed."

"Ees a coincidence, no?"

Tony stood. He opened the door and looked across the street, seeing a dark bar. He looked at the ceiling, doubting his next step. He reached into his jacket and pulled out his .38.

"Just in case, y'all hold this."

"Smart, kid. Sure thing." Zelco took the gun and slipped it into his front right pocket.

The place was definitely closed, dark and quiet. Tony looked in the peephole, a small light haloing the ring case.

"Jesus, what is it with this fucking ring?" Tony followed sports, but only to monitor his booking business. Beyond watching the occasional Saints game, he had little interest except final score and point spread. He took out the Allen wrench filed into a lockpick and popped the front door bolt.

"A bar barren of life is just a room," Tony thought, fighting off the creeps. Tony spent little time alone and would usually have some of his crew along for a job. He tried to keep quiet, but the heels on his boots knocked on the floor. He stopped, then slid like an ice skater to the ring box.

The case was hinged glass and could be smashed open. But that was inelegant, a mess that would double Alvar's reaction. If he finessed this, the dwarf may not even notice it was gone. At least for a few days.

Tony's internal alarm went off when he cracked the lock on the case. He slid to the left, a little too late. He felt his knees buckle, then he was looking at the ceiling. Alvar came into view, his encephalitic head hovering. Tony felt a rubber shoe sole pressing down on his throat.

"Tony. Fucking Tony? This ain't you. You know better." Tony reached up, gargling from the lack of air. "They sent you, right? Shit, I knew you would line up with them sooner or later. But you ain't getting that ring."

Alvar underestimated how strong Tony was, the young man having been in more fights in recent years than the bar owner. Tony chopped behind the kneecap and Alvar buckled. Tony then lifted his knees hitting his captor in the rump, throwing Alvar over his head. Tony found his feet, assuming a fighter's stance.

"How you gonna swing low, buddy?" Tony, who was over six feet, would have a hard time landing any serious punches. "You gonna fight on your knees or what?"

Alvar charged, trying to punch Tony between the legs, but the mobster anticipated the blow, sliding left and swinging the back of his fist, catching Alvar on the ear. When Alvar collapsed in pain,

Tony didn't hesitate, grabbing his collar with his left hand and the back of his shirt with the right and tossing him over the bar, where the dwarf landed with a crash. The only sound from back there was the whirring of spinning bottles.

Tony quickly opened the glass case. Pulling the ring from its velvet stand, he looked at it. It was pretty, sure, but it was like those fucking pinky rings the boys in his crew bought whenever they came into a little cash. Tony's mother would call it gaudy. He realized too late that he gave the ring too much attention.

The full force of Alvar hit Tony from behind, but the bigger man held his feet. Alvar anticipated this, climbing Tony's back like a squirrel up a tree.

"Way to throw Br'er Rabbit in the briar patch, motherfucker."

Alvar lifted a wooden handled icepick, then stabbed down, popping Tony's left eyeball like a water balloon.

With a howl more rage than pain, Tony threw his hand back and flipped Alvar over his shoulder. In an instinctive move, he kneeled on the dwarf's chest, hammering him with his right fist, which held the ring, while holding his left hand over his mangled eye.

Three, four blows rained down until Alvar found his voice.

"You gonna kill me?" Two more blows might've done just that, but Tony stopped at one. He rolled off Alvar and sat on the floor with his legs splayed, growling in pain. "Tony, I didn't mean to do that to your eye. I just wanted you to leave the ring."

Tony clambered to his knees and was about to rush Alvar, when the little man held up both of his hands.

"I'm through with all this. Take the goddamn thing. It's a curse. I ain't been laid in two years. All the cat houses won't let me in and there ain't a broad in this town that'll have me. I open up a classy place, then the fucking Blacks open theirs. They get the liquor that falls off the truck, so people go where it's cheaper. I'm barely afloat, Tony. I love that fucking thing, but I gotta get it outta here."

Tears streamed down Alvar's face. He rolled on his stomach like a pouting child, slamming his fists on the floor. Tony thought to give him another kick, but things had gone far enough. He hurried out the front door and across the street.

Tony burst into Quixote yelling that the dwarf had put his eye out. Zelco ran in back and Eula came out with towels and a first aid kit.

Tony sat in one of those ornate chairs, bending forward and groaning. He couldn't keep his good eye open, the pain searing. He felt a soft hand stroke the back of his head and another slowly lift his chin.

"Tony, baby, I gotta see. Pick that head up and let me do something before you go to the hospital."

"No hospital!" Zed slammed the table as Eula slowly lifted Tony's head and bent him back. He put his head onto the shelf of her breasts and she made no move to clear out. Eula's voice went from a soothing coo to a rasp.

"Are you fucking crazy? I ain't a nurse. He ain't gonna die over this."

"The ring!" Zed, sitting close to Tony, grasped at his right hand. Tony stopped clinching long enough to release the ring to its new owner. "Oh, my. It's mine."

"Yours?" Zelco put down a bowl filled with Everclear for sterilizing Tony's wound. "I'm sure you meant ours."

Zed had the look of grade schooler who finally got to play with the fire truck. "I meant vat I said. Bar is mine. Business is mine. You second."

"And I'm da baby brother, right? Don't remember da old country? Shit you ain't said since we're teens? Now it comes up?"

"It comes up cause you talk out of turn."

"I'm cutta turn? You drop this crazy talk and I'm outta turn?"

Now that she had cleaned up the blood, Eula taped five layers of gauze over the eye, then helped Tony to his feet. Zed stepped over, grabbing Eula by the shoulders and shaking her.

"Vat I tell you? You go novhere."

Tony dropped back into the chair and saw Zelco reach into his coat pocket.

"Getcha hands off my daughter." He pointed Tony's pistol at his brother.

"Now who act crazy, boy? We let him go, we maybe lose ring."

Zed zipped towards his brother and grasped for his wrist. Zelco tried to pull back.

"Stop, Zelco. You vill listen."

"Don't fucking touch me."

The two rotund men wrestled on the floor. Eula helped Tony stand and led him to the door. As Eula went to push it open, they both jumped as the pistol cracked. Zelco stood over a prone Zed.

Tony's brain felt a jolt of recognition and he ran to Zelco, pushing him with both hands.

"Fuck, that's my gun! You gonna pin this on me?"

Zelco dropped to his knees and held the pistol butt up to Tony.

"No! I didn't ... I didn't think, Tony."

"You damn right you didn't. I ain't going nowhere 'til you make this right."

Zelco wiped the tears from his eyes, bumping the palms of his hands on his forehead. "Okay, okay. I guess I'm in charge now. I'll make you second. In a few years, you get the whole thing."

"How do I know this?"

"I'll make you my son-in-law. Eula needs to get married."

"You can't guarantee that."

"Don't speak so fast, Tony." Eula wrapped her arm around his waist. "Maybe we can talk about this on the way to the hospital."

Eula helped Tony to the door.

"Eula, I gotta say something. I ain't married, but I gotta kid."

"Easy, Tony. We just talking." The two left as Zelco wondered how the hell to get rid of the body.

PART TWO: SLIPPING AT MICKEY'S

Was there anything worse than the goddamn white suits?

Seegar looked at his fatigue coat, black t-shirt and bell-bottomed jeans and felt underdressed. Here he was, back in New Orleans, back in Metairie, back in Fat fucking City for crying out loud, and still there were Travolta wannabes who'd seen "Saturday Night Fever" and ran to Chess King to suit up.

Wasn't this town timeless? Hirt and Fountain on Bourbon, Mardi Gras balls, that sort of shit? No, it was still the '70s, whether he liked it or not.

He'd heard Macallister's Landing was the hip new place, but it would take something different than a deejay dropping those same Bee Gees songs to impress him. The club was too hot, too smoky and too much, so he went outside to the courtyard for some quiet.

Outdoors was enclosed by a wooden fence and a faux bamboo roof covered the bar for those rainy afternoons, no doubt. The barstools were wooden and looked uncomfortable, but he took one anyway, as the blonde bartender, hair feathering out from a middle part, made her way over. She pointed at him.

"Baby, this is disco night. 'Taxi Driver' night is later on."

"Didn't come for the music. Was hoping for a cold tap beer."

"I can do that."

"Tap's the way to go." Seegar turned and saw a long-haired young man whose blonde bangs fell to the top of his eyes. Tamping his cigarette, he held out a hand. "Felix."

They shook. Felix jerked a thumb toward the club.

"Don't worry about those fucks. They clear out on Saturday

night."

"Why?"

"Because my band plays here. And those creeps don't like Zeppelin."

"Shit, I think I should come out for that."

"Fuckin' A, bra. Hope to see you then." He slammed back the rest of his beer and gave Seegar the up-nod before heading out the door. The bartender brought Seegar his own red plastic cup.

"They any good?"

The bartender nodded enthusiastically.

"Oh yeah. They're called Zebra and they do some Zep, some Rush, you know. I once got them to do 'Paranoid,' but Randy don't like singing Ozzie."

"Sounds like my kinda scene."

"Better than this shit, that's for sure." She pointed at one polyester shirt showing another polyester shirt how to do The Hustle.

"It's the worst thing out," Seegar said. She looked shocked.

"You from here?"

"Why?"

"Well, my mama used to say that same thing. But I ain't never seen you around."

"My mom said it too. I was born here, but I haven't been down in a long time. Glad to be back, though."

"Permanent?"

"Permanent." She smiled and held out her hand.

"My name's Seely."

"Mine's Seegar."

"Wow, it's almost like the same name. That's weird."

An older man came from inside. Slipping behind the bar, he pulled some bills out of the register and dropped in two rolls of quarters. He had a gut, but his shoulders and arms showed a rounded strength. As he walked back inside, Seegar scanned the wood paneled back wall and caught sight of a gold ring in a plastic case, a gaudy creation littered with fake diamonds.

"What the hell is that?"

"You ever hear of Paul Hornung?" She pointed to the poster above the ring.

"Sure." He now recognized old Golden Boy in the poster. It was an older shot of him in a Notre Dame jersey instead of Green Bay.

"That's his Super Bowl ring. He gave it to Mr. Black who used to have a bar up the street. When that place closed, he gave it to my dad."

"Gave it?"

"Well, loaned it. It's his whenever he wants it. We get a few people in here who just want to stare at it. It's good for a few beers."

Seegar looked at his watch, then finished up his draft.

"You got someplace to be?"

"In the morning. I just wanted a quick cold one."

The older man returned with three unopened bottles of Jack Daniels.

"Daddy, meet the new guy in town."

The old man smiled without showing teeth, holding out his mitt. "Norton."

"I'm Seegar." The young man felt the tight grip go slack, along with the smile on the older man's face.

"You ain't from here?"

"Born but not raised."

The old man gave Seegar a glottal "Hmph" while nodding.

"Nice meeting y'all. I'll be back for Saturday night."

Seegar walked up Edenborn to the apartment he had moved into earlier that day. The concrete block didn't seem like New Orleans living, but it was cheap and it was available. It was home, for now.

Seegar thought this neighborhood was pretty loud for a Thursday night. Every bar had music seeping from the walls, people fuming cigarette smoke while hanging out on patios, knocking back plastic cups of beer and cocktails. He passed a group of 30ish guys with graying mustaches who reeked of bourbon. One guy held up a plastic cup half-lined with amber.

"Come on, baby. You in Fat City. I saw you shake your head. I can drink anywhere I want."

"That's cool."

"That's New Orleans." He chugged the rest of his drink, dropping the cup in the middle of the street. Seegar watched it settle into the crook of the steel gutter grate, its last few drops dribbling out to Lake Pontchartrain.

He climbed the steps in the building, the center opening ten stories to the roof. The locks of his third floor pad snapped open and he pushed in the heavy industrial door to see nothing but brown carpet and the duffel bag filled with everything he possessed from a two-year Army stint. He had pushed it up against the wall under a window sealed off from the world by plastic Venetian blinds. Stripping down to his olive green boxers, he reclined on the bare floor, head sinking into the bag, and stared at the pebbled ceiling as sleep started to take over his brain.

"Well, I sorta met a girl. I guess I sorta got to get a job."

The warehouse was a three-car garage with a tiny apartment on top, cars protected by a roll-down aluminum shutter. Since the place was on Hessmer, only a few blocks from his building, Seegar strolled over there after having a coffee at the Time Saver. Everything around here was either those blocky apartment buildings or squat concrete bricks holding businesses.

Seegar blanched a bit before hitting the doorbell, but he rang it anyway.

"What?" The hollow voice barked out of the little box.

"Mr. Murano?"

The line between the two men stayed open, but the guy upstairs stayed silent.

"My name is Seegar Reingold. I think you knew my mother."

The line hung up, but the clanking chains wound up the garage door. Tony Murano stood over his head, looking down from an office door.

"Yeah, you're Judy's kid. Come on up."

Seegar bounded up the stairs, the metallic steps bonging with his heavy stride.

Tony was already seated when Seegar stepped into the office. The older man pointed at a red chair and Seegar sat.

"I didn't know you was coming, but I know why you're here."

"It was one of the last things Mom ever said."

"I take last words very seriously. But I will have to ask: is there any reason why I can't trust you?"

"Yeah."

"That was quick."

"I don't believe in dancing around."

"Good. Now call the tune."

"The Army considers me dishonorable."

"That could be considered a bad thing. Is there an authority problem?"

"Well, I hate the government."

"You ain't alone."

Seegar stifled a laugh by dragging his thumb across his nose. "Look, Mr. Murano. Tony ..."

Tony's eyebrows arched into commas, all the more disturbing because the eye patch moved with the change in expression. Seegar tried to keep focused on the good eye.

"Mr. Murano, the Army has a lot of tells. They tell you when to eat, when to sleep and when to shit. They tell you what to wear and how to wear it. They tell you how long your hair can be down to the millimeter. They tell you what constitutes clean and that never includes having a piece of bubblegum. I'm hoping we only have two tells. You tell me what to do and I tell you I got it done."

"What's your rifle ranking?"

"Sharpshooter. Missed marksman by two points."

Tony picked up the phone, spinning its rotary wheel as fast as he could.

"Hildy, you're gonna pick up someone for your rounds tomorrow. Yeah, new guy. Give him the tour."

Seely rolled over to meet the day. Downstairs was bright with natural light. Norton was still entombed in his blacked-out bedroom, as he never went to bed before 5 a.m. and rarely saw the light side of 4 p.m. Some days, he would sleep at the bar on an old day bed, a habit dating back to his marriage and its occasional rocky shores. An old night owl, he called himself. She thought it was also true because he watched everything all the time.

She was young, not requiring as much sack time as the big guy. Besides, the good soap opera started at noon.

She put some water on the boil and pulled the yellow Community coffee bag out of the fridge. Norton only let her use the old ceramic pot, not getting her the Mr. Coffee she begged for, but the chicory sharpness of the dark roast was there whether it was automatic or not.

After two cups heavily creamed with half and half, she slipped on her tan crocheted bikini and stepped out to the pool. A chilly hook hung in the air, but the sun was out and now was the perfect time to trade milky winter skin for summery cafe au lait.

"Best to get some sun without the sweat," she thought, imagining the film of humidity soon to cover her world.

After a quick splash, she slicked her hair back and stared up at the blue sky. Blue, like the water in the pool. Like that Seegar's eyes.

"That's another swim I'd like to take."

Seely thought back to what her dad said right after Seegar left the bar. "I don't like the looks of him."

Her father had never said that before and she wondered where it came from. She decided she didn't care and hoped the new guy would show up for some Zebra.

Hildy drove a GTO, a '68 with the hidden headlights with the original red color. It rumbled like a rolling earthquake under Seegar's seat, as he felt the power of the engine even when crawling slowly through the side streets of Fat City.

"Is it tough to keep this puppy reigned in?"

Hildy turned down the radio. She had been blasting WRNO and the Beatles song that the deejay, Michael In the Morning, spun.

"It's actually running a little rough right now. I'm gonna break open the carburetor this weekend and see if it needs work. This one has the Ram Air II, so it should move like lightning. Right now, it just rumbles like thunder."

"I have no idea what you're talking about."

"I guess you weren't in the motor pool, huh?"

"I can type 90 words per minute."

"Macho."

Hildy laughed, sounding more like a neigh. She looked to Seegar's eyes like the perfect pilot for the muscle car, rangy as a greyhound and just as taught. Her nose sloped to a wide mouth and her midnight hair fell in thick bangs just past her eyebrows, like Chrissy Hinds' hair over Carly Simon's face. She wore a black motorcycle jacket and a white t-shirt with boyish jeans covering black leather engineer boots. If you could make a car into a centaur from those Greek stories, Hildy and this Goat would make one incredible steed

"You work on this thing yourself?"

"I get under there every weekend. I can't help poking around."

"You're like The Fonz, right? Except female."

"I hope that means I'm cool."

Seegar kept his mouth shut. Hildy waited as long as she could, looking from the street to him and back four times before she laughed again.

"Yeah," she said. "Let's get to it."

As she looked back to the road, Seegar glanced at her face. She was cool, he thought. So many women put up a gate, separating them from the attention of men. They made everything a dance and Seegar never knew if he was supposed to two-step, jig or second line. But Hildy was relaxed, a woman used to having men around. There was little nuance to what she said and her dagger sharpness made Seegar fall right in line with what would surely be a series of orders.

She took a right on a wide street and drove towards Veterans Blvd.

"This is Severn, the boundary line. To the left, Mr. Navia runs things all the way to Chalmette, including the Quarter. Pop's business goes to Green Acres."

Seegar barely knew these suburban streets, but it sounded like this Navia guy controlled the whole city. Tony had carved himself a thin slice of the pie.

She turned right on Veterans, gunning the motor.

"Shit, what is that sticking?" Seegar felt nothing. "Anyway, we cross the interstate all the way to Airline. We got a few of those hot sheet motels out there, but we keep out of Shrewsbury where the blacks are. Too many guns and not enough money. Basically, any bar around Fat City and New Metairie pays us to make sure nothing goes wrong, the right people drink there and the supply lines stay open."

"That's a wide range of service."

"It can be. Some places like the cheap booze that comes in the top shelf labels. Some like a shoebox full of eight balls and a few bottles of 'ludes for their special customers. Every once in a while we'll get some junk if someone has the cash for it, but we keep that stuff rare."

"Because of the cops?"

"We have an understanding with the beat boys. The sheriff is a real hard ass, so we can't go too far with anything. Okay, first stop."

She pulled into the driveway of a very small bar that looked closed, but Hildy strode right in. She walked like she drove, forward with no hesitation, an unstoppable force in a yielding world.

For the next three hours, Seegar met a series of fat balding men in their 40s and 50s whose lives were lived in the few feet behind a bar, pleasant open faces reflecting a lifetime of hearing the same five stories and the same twenty songs on the juke. They were listeners instead of talkers, a lay priesthood ready in their confessional for the lonely, tired and horny. Cigarette smoke was their incense and bottles of altar wine stood ready for nightly communion.

They had a quick smile for Hildy with a quick move to the wrinkled and full manila folder that she traded for an equally wrinkled but empty one. She took orders without ever taking notes and introduced Seeger by saying, "You'll be seeing him instead of me real soon." They accepted it with a nod.

Just after noon, she pulled into another bar on Veterans called The Swamp Room.

"They got a grill in here. You want a burger?"

Seegar agreed and they stepped in. This place was bigger than most of the joints they'd been to: back room with a row of dart boards, a walled-off pool table at the end of the front bar and enough room near the front door for a half-dozen four-top tables. Hildy pulled up a barstool, the padded kind with a backrest, and Seegar sat beside her as the bartender came up. For the first time all day, he did not greet Hildy by her first name.

"We're looking to get some lunch," Hildy said. "I hear you got a good burger."

"The best." The bartender put both hands on the wood and spread out like a proud papa.

"You got fries with that?"

"Yeah. Steak fries."

"Cool. Two burgers. How you want yours cooked?"

"Well."

Hildy shook her head as if he'd told a joke. "What, are you a redneck? Jesus. Okay, one medium rare and one burnt. And two Dixies to drink." Seegar had never tried this kind of beer, but didn't question his new boss. The bottles arrived near frozen and he took a sip. It was like most other beers, but its sugary finish tasted wrong.

"You'll get used to it," Hildy said as he made a face. "In fact, you'll soon crave it."

"We'll see."

"Make you a bet. If that ain't your beer of choice in three months, I'll let you have the car. For a day, not for good."

"What do I have to do?"

"Nothing. I just have a feeling."

"Deal."

Hildy picked up the bottle, motioning for him to stay put while she toured the place. There were a couple of mustachioed and weak-chinned guys popping the pool balls, but the place was otherwise empty. "Take This Job and Shove It," that Johnny Paycheck song you couldn't avoid if you wanted, played on the jukebox. Hildy sat back down.

"God, I hate country."

"Yeah. Luckily only a few people listen to it." Seegar had his fill of the music during basic training, as every shitkicker in his unit blasted Nashville.

"You don't like that disco crap, huh?"

"Naw."

"Good. If you're gonna work with me, you gotta like to rock."

"Hey, how are those Zebra guys?"

"Pretty good. I mean, they think they're gonna be like Zepplin or something, but they won't ever leave New Orleans."

"Still, a good time?"

"Yeah. Macallister's."

"On Saturday, I know. Felix told me about it."

"He's cool. But I could fuck the shit out of Randy." Seegar stopped himself from spitting out his beer. "I mean, so could every Fat City chick. Just grab that hair, pull him down and grind." She shook all over as if she was doing it right that second.

"What do you think of Seely?"

"Oh, she's great." Hildy's screwed up her face. "You mean like friends, right? Not something weird."

"Yeah, yeah."

"Okay. Had me worried there. So, I guess you like her."

"I've spent all of ten minutes with her. But that was a damn good start."

"Cool. Well, she ain't got a boyfriend."

"Very, very cool."

The bartender placed two Styrofoam plates in front of them, each containing a burger the size of a baseball cap and fries in the remaining space.

"Wow, this looks great." Hildy nodded as the bartender slid bottles of ketchup and mustard in front of his customers. They ate in silence, Hildy wiping her mouth of juicy runoff while Seegar enjoyed the crisp char of the flame-cooked meat. He loaded his plate with ketchup for the fries, but she abstained.

"I like to taste the potato. Just salt and pepper is all I need."

"Army food is so goddamn bad, you have to drench it in something. Ketchup, A-1, Heinz 57. Anything to give it some flavor." As he ate the final fry, Hildy's face focused, moving nose to nose.

"My back. You got it?"

"Yeah."

"Just follow my lead."

The bartender came over. "Anything else? Another beer?"

"No, that's it."

"That'll be $7.50."

"I don't think so." While the bartender tried to figure out what she meant, Hildy stood and pulled a .45 from inside her jacket in one single sweep. Seegar saw one of the pool players make a move to the payphone. He slammed the guy's head into the wall with a forearm. Hildy cocked the gun. "I know you're new here, buddy, but you need to take some advice. Tony Murano calls you for a meeting, you take it. Period."

She fired repeatedly, aiming left and right. Bottles exploded like watery fireworks. She jerked her thumb at Seegar and they ran out of the place, leaving the bartender on the floor in a pool of booze, broken glass and his own piss.

Hildy screeched the Goat onto Vets, causing an El Camino full of pool cleaning supplies to fishtail. But, while her eyes remained focused and serious, her mouth barked out her laughter.

"Hoo, baby, right into the deep end, huh?"

"Wow, did all the guys have to go through this?"

"What guys?"

"The other people who work for your father."

"Shit, are you serious? Dad hasn't brought on somebody new in five years."

"Really?"

"Who was the last one he brought on?"

"Me."

Hildy slowed as she saw two Jefferson Parish sheriff cars whoop their way in the other direction. The 40-foot wide drainage canal running down the center of the street kept them insulated from attention. She blew out a deep breath, seeming to relax. Seegar saw something soft crease her eyes, her greyhound face looking puppyish for the first time since they met.

"So, you're all your old man needs?"

"Probably."

"Then why me?"

She pulled into the warehouse. "Ain't nothing cuter than a stray, boo. But they're also the most loyal."

Seegar laughed to show he was a good sport, but it stung. Orphans, like stray puppies, don't like to be kicked. But Tony smiled wide when Seegar came into the room.

"He done good?"

Hildy nodded. "Real good."

"Police band was blowing up. I'll have to wet the sergeant's beak, but it'll pay off when that guy is added to the route. He will pay, won't he?"

Seegar stepped up before Hildy could answer. "If he wants to stay in business."

Tony put his right hand on Seegar's left shoulder.

"Yeah, kid. And now, you can call me Tony." Tony slapped him on the back. "But Mr. Tony. Like a good Metairie boy."

"Yes, sir, Mr. Tony."

"Hildy, take him for a drink."

They went to The Front Page, the last bar on their route. She ordered two Dixies and he drank the beer slowly, because it really tasted bad.

"Okay, next week you get a car."

"A Goat?"

"You wish. I think we got a Thunderbird."

"Shit, those boats?"

"You can't ride a bike and do this job."

"What if I get a banana seat?"

"Idiot. Seriously, until you make some green, you're on welfare. That okay?"

"Define green."

"Five percent of every pickup you make. Flat fee for every task above and beyond."

"Cool."

"Okay. You get this weekend off so I can work out the car." She slipped him a folded-up stash of bills. "Here's a taste for today. Go make some groceries. We'll see you at the warehouse bright and early Monday." She stood up and punched his shoulder. "Alright, I'm gonna go get laid. I suggest you do the same."

Before he could turn around, she was gone.

He finished the beer, getting change for a dollar. He walked up to Veterans, catching the bus down to Dorignac's Grocery and, when he returned to Fat City, he had a pound of sliced ham, a dozen eggs, a sheath of Bunny Bread, two steaks, red new potatoes, a head of iceberg lettuce and some Marie's Bleu Cheese Dressing. He felt that should cover him until Monday when he could drive wherever he wanted to go.

By the time he got back to his apartment, the sun had gone down, but the cool sapphire glow of dusk had yet to succumb to night. He broiled the steak and boiled the potatoes, cut a wedge of lettuce, dousing it in sauce, eating until he was satisfied. He stepped out onto his patio, tired of staring at the wall.

He had eaten standing up in the kitchen because he still had no place to sit except the floor. As he looked into night, he thought he may catch a movie at Lakeside Mall. But his thoughts turned blonde and a thirst for draft beer overcame him.

"I guess I don't wait for Saturday," he thought and went to take a shower.

Seely had gotten to the bar around three. On Fridays, Norton opened the place at noon, but that was an excuse for him to restock and clean while selling a few to his hardcore regulars. Her job was to get the place through Happy Hour and early evening, maybe sticking around to help if they were slammed.

The daddy-daughter combo worked the indoor bar together through a brisk after-work crowd. Young pros who worked at the banks along Vets wearing their thick argyle ties and leisure suits liked to preen for the blow-dried secretaries in their loose fitting blouses and tight-fitting polyester slacks. The ancient mating dance, now fueled with wine spritzers and Harvey Wallbangers with the occasional spoon of coke, continued unabated as Macallister's filled with the cloying aroma of sweaty arousal.

Seely stayed outside the herd, more wrangler than willing participant. While she wore clothes designed to fill up the tip jar, like tonight's Jordache jeans, so tight she couldn't wear panties, and a tied-up shirt to reveal her belly, she always cut off any flirtation before the customer could even think he had a shot. Focused like an owl perched above the scuttling squirrels, she watched the ebb and flow of one male boogieing up to one female, knowing immediately if rejection or acceptance would come, followed by the scan and scout of interest lost and gained. While she hated this disco music, especially when real rocking dudes like Kiss or Rod Stewart felt the need to worship at its altar, she could see how the funky drums could drive this generation's need to make babies.

By the time the Happy Hour crowd had moved on to dinners or house parties or whatever else the city had to offer, Seely felt drained. Once one person ordered a fancy drink, there would be a run with each different guy trying to out-cute the other. She had made grasshoppers, piña coladas, white Russians, margaritas, anything blended and served with fruit. At eight p.m., with only a couple of hours left before she finished up, she had little left for the remaining few.

But then that guy from last night walked in and she was lifted out of the muck.

Seegar saw Seely's mouth grow into a toothy smile and he warmed in the fire of attention. He also felt a bit self-conscious since he was dressed exactly the same as the night before.

"I took your advice and got a job as a taxi driver today." Seely giggled. "So, if tonight is taxi driver night ..."

"I think taxi driver night is whenever you come in." Norton walked behind Seely, and she knew she was being watched. She dropped her smile and said, "Beer?"

Seegar pulled back from the bar, realizing how far he was leaning over it. He nodded and pulled up a seat. When the door to the back room shut, Seely leaned back over.

"Babe, my daddy don't like you."

"That'd make me really upset if I was thirteen and I wanted to ask you to the homecoming dance."

She withdrew a bit, but the smile was back.

"He ain't always like this."

"It's too bad."

"Yeah."

"Cause, y'know, I'm always like this." He took off his jacket and leaned forward, doing his best to flex muscles built by basic training.

Norton lumbered out and saw the two of them far closer than he wanted.

"Is this guy gonna drink?"

"He ordered a beer."

"Then maybe he should actually have one." He locked eyes with Seegar. "And he should pay for it."

She went over to the tap. "Hey, we have Dixie."

"Anything else, please."

He took the draft and went to one of the back tables. He watched the place fill up and the other bartenders filter in. After half an hour, Norton traded the cash registrar drawers, taking the full one to the back. Seely switched out a few bottles, then poured a draft. She put it on a bar tray and walked it to Seegar.

She put down a napkin and then the draft, but the cup didn't cover the white paper. He picked it up.

"Meet me in Drago's parking lot in one hour."

Back behind bar, Seeley filled a cup with ice, spritzing club soda almost to the top and shaking in four dashes of Peychaud bitters. As the drink took on a purple hue, she took it to the back office.

"Hey, I'm almost done here." Norton's pencil swirled through his ledger.

She placed the cup on the desk. "Cool, but I'm not gonna go home just yet."

He took a long swig and gave her a disapproving look.

"No, dad."

"No what?"

"No, I'm not meeting him. He's cute, but the city is full of other people. Like Mimi, who I made plans with earlier."

"Fine. But I really mean what I said about him."

"I heard you," she said. But she thought, "I ain't listening."

Drago's was only a few blocks away, like everything else in Fat City. Seegar waited for ten minutes as he watched the bus boys and cooks leave the triangle-roofed restaurant. He turned back towards Macallister's, seeing Seely walk up.

Maybe it was the moonlight that cast sharp shadows across her body accentuating her trim figure. Maybe it was the halogen street lamps that haloed her face, making her look angelic. Or maybe it was the simple fact that Seely was one of the most beautiful women Seegar had ever seen and she smiled when their eyes locked. But one thing was sure: Seegar felt for the first time since his mom had died that maybe this shit storm of a life was gonna reveal some sunshine.

"Hey, sailor, you looking for a date?"

"Soldier, actually."

"Ah. The jacket makes sense now."

"The jacket makes some sense, yes. And I am."

"You are what?"

"Looking for a date."

"Then you're in luck. Because I have a couple of hours I can give you. But it ain't free."

Seegar knew she was joking, but had learned a long time ago that nothing came without a price. "Whatever it takes."

"I thought you'd say that. Let's walk."

Together they crossed Severn, walking past the Lakeside Mall movie theater. The last show had just let out and a bustle of teenagers lounged on the front steps trying to figure out what they wanted to do before it got too late. Seegar and Seely slipped into the empty parking lot where the lights had been turned off.

"Here's the deal," she said, pulling him to a halt and turning him, wanting to stare into his eyes. "For some reason, my dad doesn't want you and me to be around each other."

"I got that."

"I figured, but what you don't got is that I'm too well known in our little corner of the world for us to be seen together. If we go to the Fat City bars, dimes will be dropping as fast as slot machines."

"I get a car on Monday."

"That's a good start. But here's the thing. I depend on my dad for rides, a bedroom, my job. It's hard for me to get out of his sight."

"Like tonight."

"Yeah. I think he knows damn well I ain't drinking with Mimi. But he also knows I will do as he says if there's any chance of me getting caught."

"Let me work on that. I bet we can come up with something."

"You better. Because if you don't, tonight's the only night I'll ever come out and play." She undid the bottom knot of her blouse and flashed him two bra-covered B-cups straight out of a glossy porn magazine. "Now, where do you live exactly?"

After a quick stop at the Time Saver for a pack of rubbers, Seegar trying not to run to get there, they finally made back to his apartment.

Seely rolled her eyes as they walked in.

"How long have you been here?"

"Five days."

"After you get a car, you might want to get a bed."

"As soon as I can."

Seegar unrolled his sleeping bag as wide as he could and soon they were rolling around on each other, lips and tongues finding precious nooks where deep pressure turned into deep pleasure. Seely stood, kicking off her clogs. She undid the two buttons that clasped her shirt, revealing one of those new bras that wrapped around her neck instead of her shoulders. She pulled the top strap over her head, turning her back to Seegar as she unhooked the bottom. She held the cups to her breasts, bending over to let her cleavage waterfall in front of his eyes, until she dropped the lace onto his face. As she stood back up, fully and gloriously exposed, she examined the crotch of his pants.

"I see the little soldier is standing at attention."

"Sir, yes, sir." He saluted.

As she peeled the tight jeans from her bare rear, a red ring in her flesh where the waistband had embedded itself, Seegar smiled.

"What?"

"That's something I never thought I would see."

She really hoped he didn't mean a pussy.

"You're a natural blonde."

She rubbed her pubic mound.

"Yeah. I am."

"Me too."

"So show me."

Seely unzipped his jeans. Grabbing both the waist of the pants and the band of his jockey shorts, she tugged down. Bushing about an erect cock was flaxen hair very close to her color.

"There you go," she said. "Ain't we a couple of rare birds."

In the flash of a few seconds, eyes flickered up and down glimmering skin to collect the information that, yes, they were both now naked and, yes, they were going to do something with that. The second passed, mental images stored, and the immersion began.

Now, in addition to lips and tongues, they added hands to the explorations, finding aching crevices below the waist, like the angle of hip along the abs-buttocks line where a thumb could grind hard into flesh. There was also the top of the hamstring just below the ass cheek where a cupped hand could pull upwards, releasing a shaking spasm of energy.

And those breasts. Seegar manipulated them upwards, side to side, coaxed them downward as she hovered above him, anything to feel that silken flesh play across his hands, his face and his chest. Finally, he sheathed himself in rubber and slowly pushed himself in.

In little more than five strokes, he exploded, unable to stop the overwhelming tide of his pleasures. He bounded to his feet and ran into the bathroom, emerging with a hand towel around his crotch.

Seely, incensed, decided to be nice about this, but never see this asshole again.

"Hey, it happens to everyone, right?"

Seegar had been distracted in his cleaning up.

"What do you mean?" He pulled the towel away to reveal an erect and sperm-free penis.

"Nothing," she said, as he put on another condom and dove back in.

After twenty minutes of pushing and holding, Seely's legs going wide, up and clinched around his back, she climbed on top. He bridged his back, lifting her off the floor, this extra pressure digging him in deep enough to press the button. He dropped back down and she ground her hips and knees until a shuddering starting in her ankles rippled until it shot out of the top of her head. The primal and guttural moan accompanying the orgasm frightened Seegar. It had been almost six months since he had last visited this magical land of sex, but never before had he made it his home.

Seely's sweaty collapse on Seegar's chest nearly knocked the air out of him. He reveled in her moist skin, drawing her close. She reached down, pulling the rubber from him, and tugged until her hand was sticky and his flesh was limp. They lay there for nearly a minute trying to understand what this ferocity could mean, because neither had been this good with anyone else ever. Period.

Five minutes passed staring at the ceiling, letting their hearts run down to normal. Seely grabbed the towel, trying to clean her hand. This led to the shower, which soon became an excuse for tits and dick to become very clean. Finally, dressed in the warm clothes, Seely looked at her watch. One a.m., time for her to head back to the bar and lie to her father that she and Mimi were done.

Seegar saw her to the door in his jockeys. After one last kiss, which was really about twenty wrapped into one, she backed out of the transom.

"Find a way to make this work. Just … just fucking do it."

Seegar slept, which meant rolling around for forty-five minute spurts, roiling dreams firing his brain. He decided around noon to quit pretending. The thoughts of a cheeseburger and fries took the sting out of his zombified disposition and he wandered into the streets of Fat City to feed himself.

Fed yet still grumpy, he walked past the Murano warehouse. Tony's car wasn't around, but Hildy's GTO was. He pushed the doorbell.

Hildy was working on the car, but had gone upstairs to cool off. She sat in her father's chair, black Chuck Taylors on the blotter.

"Hey, dude. I ain't got you a car yet."

"That's okay. I just wanted to hang."

"Could you give me a hand?"

"Do my best."

They went downstairs as Hildy got dirty and Seegar tried not to get in the way. After a few minutes of work, Seegar unloaded his troubles on his new boss.

"You got yourself a pickle there, boy."

"Yeah. Shit ain't pretty."

"You know, I dig Seely. She's always been cool to me."

"That's good."

"She and I have a few daddy issues, as you can tell."

"You mean Tony keeps you on a short lease?"

"I moved out as soon as I could. His wife is not my mom."

"Bummer."

"Ah, she's okay. Dad really loves her, so I decided to get out of the way. So, Norton?"

"I have no idea why he's against me."

"He used to work for my dad, y'know. Maybe he doesn't want a lawless character like you for his princess."

"He doesn't know what I do. Seely neither. Unless your dad spilled."

"I do all the runs. Pop can't be bothered. He don't see hardly anyone anymore."

"Then this doesn't make any sense."

"The way I see it, man, we got love at first sight, right?"

"Love is a strong word. Lust is better."

"Okay, lust at first sight, jackass. And then we got hate at first sight. You don't seem like the type to be in the middle of that."

"I draw trouble. I'm a goddamn magnet."

Hildy carefully removed the carburetor, then wiped a line of grease right across her forehead. "I can help. Meet me back here at six. Now get the fuck out my way."

She jerked her thumb. He drifted home to get some real sleep.

After dropping down deep and shaking off the darkness that had been creeping around his edges, Seeger did a round of calisthenics to get his heart pumping, then showered. He slipped on his last clean t-shirt and the same jeans, then walked back to the warehouse.

Hildy was back in the office. She had also cleaned up, but still wore her white tee and jeans.

"You need to get some new clothes, man."

"You're one to talk."

"Guys don't seem to care, but girls might not be forgiving."

"Duly noted. I'll solve that problem when I can hold on to the woman I have."

"Speaking of which ..." Hildy pulled out a sandwich bag full of white powder. "This should be the solution."

"Whoa, coke ain't for me."

"It ain't coke. And it ain't for you. It's chloral hydrate. You know, mickey finn."

"What?"

"Jesus! Don't you know anything? Mix with this alcohol and you got a no-smell, no-mess knockout drop."

"This could work."

"I know Norton. Every night, he has bitters and soda while he does the books. Tell Seely to set aside a special bottle just for dear old Dad and you two can have some fun knowing you won't get caught." Seegar picked up the bag. "Make sure she knows, man. Three drops. No more. And, this is important, this is a personal favor from me to you. Nobody knows where you got it. Especially my old man."

Seegar put the baggie in his pocket.

"Is this that *omerta* I heard so much about?"

"No, it's a favor. Jesus, you're a jackass." She barked. "Just because we're Italian don't make us the mob."

"And here I was thinking I might become the Godfather. Is there any future at all?"

"You keep thinking, Seegar. With practice, you just might get it right."

Norton was as happy as he was gonna be. The books were tight, Seely kept her hand out of the till, and, for now, so were the bartenders, as they were too new to steal just yet. He'd know when they started.

The band was finishing up, doing another one of those Led Zeppelin songs. Norton couldn't tell one from the other, only that Randy's voice went into an ever higher register, a fucking eagle screech to him. Norton wished there was another like Louis Prima around and that people would pay to see him.

Seely walked in, carrying his goodnight cocktail.

"Here ya go," she said and kissed him on the top of the head.

"Thanks, baby. I'm closing you out ... now."

One last mark in his ledger, he handed her a small manila folder with her tips. He always dropped in another fiver because she was keeping him in business. The day she got a boyfriend may be the day his business died.

"Hey, Mimi wants to talk. Told her I'd buy her a burger at The Swamp Room."

"Here." He held out his car keys. "You know those girls will keep these rock stars drinking until four."

"Cool, I'll come pick you up when I'm done."

She rubbed his shoulders and he took a long swig. It was ironic, he thought, quitting drinking just when he bought a bar. He didn't need to, more of a want. He saw those rag pushers in their four stool joints barely getting by. No, this was a business and hands off of the stock.

But as he got older, his stomach went south on him. Someone told him bitters and soda was an easy way to combat it. Can't really get drunk on a few shakes of liquor, but it helped him shave off the edge. Something to relax him. Something to help him sleep. He finished this cup and felt it go to work.

Seely walked out of the office feeling wrong. This was over the line, some real evil shit like a voodoo curse or calling on the devil. But wasn't he the one that was being evil too? Norton said a million times that her being available made the tips double. And, after just one look, he thought he might lose her forever? The hell with it, she thought. He'll come around soon enough. When, or at least if, he sees her happy with him, there won't be anything to do but accept facts.

"Goddamn," she said out loud. "Bastard better be worth it."

One hour later, they lay on their stomachs, each trying to figure out if the other wanted to rub skin one more time before Seeley went back to the bar in time to wake up her father. Slick from exertion and Seeley's hair matted with sweat, Seegar couldn't stand it anymore, slipping closer to connect all their angles into one being.

"Enjoy it, boy. We won't be back here again."

They lay in Seely's room, tension of the forbidden released. She kicked off the covers and stood up, trying to cool off.

"I told you. I'm getting a bed tomorrow."

"Bed, car, new clothes. It's like you won the sweepstakes or something."

"Sort of."

His eyes locked onto her nakedness. She felt the weight of his gaze and turned without actually putting any clothes on. "Stop it."

"Can't."

"I don't like it."

"I do. I like it a lot."

He stood and posed across the bed. "C'mon. You try it." He flourished his hands up and down like one of those model chicks on "The Price Is Right." "Get a good look at all this."

She looked him over, crossing her arms over her nipples.

"Looks good, soldier. But did I tell you at ease?"

He fiddled with his flaccidity to stretch it back out.

"Gimme a break. You telling me all the guys you been with have my kind of stamina?"

"No, you're impressive."

"Thanks. Besides, are you at attention after all that?"

She looked at the cleavage created by her arms, then whipped them out like wings.

"Ten-hut." He clapped softly. "I'm nowhere near the soldier you are."

"Don't know about that," she said and saw him stirring. What he thought was dead had risen again. "But we don't have time for another. Save it for tomorrow."

He watched her go into the bathroom and pull on her panties. He gathered together his scattered duds and made himself decent.

In her car on the way back to Macallister's, Seely locked down on the road in front of them. He felt her avoiding his gaze.

"I mean ..." She tried to get started, but choked on her words.

"I'm listening," he said, squeezing her thigh.

"I know people. I mean, I know a lot of people. The more I think about it, I can't see how we can get away with this."

"Don't quite see what you mean."

"Y'know, fucking is quite good. But we'll get bored eventually. And I just can't be seen with you."

"You mean in Fat City?"

"Where the fuck else would I mean?"

"Well, we could go down to the Quarter or something."

"The Quarter? Nobody goes all the way down to the Quarter."

"Yeah. Nobody goes down to the Quarter."   She shook her head, the mask of concentration falling between her legs. "Yeah, it's like all of twenty minutes away. We'd have to find parking or something."

They started laughing together until she choked.

"Oh shit," she said. "I guess my world is pretty small."

"Yeah. I been all the way to San Diego. I got what they call perspective. Plus, all the guys talked about Bourbon Street."

"Yeah. I never go there."

"I guess you are now."

"I guess I am."

They locked fingers across her armrest. When they got to his apartment building, it took him fifteen minutes to get out of the car. She finally had to accelerate away to stop worrying that Norton may know exactly what was going on.

But she found him napping on his office bed. Checking to make sure all of the books were done, she shook him awake.

"You have a good time?"

"It was alright."

He stood up and they went home.

Sunday was a day of rest. Norton always insisted on going to mass at St. Angela Merici, so Seely donned a dress and nice pumps. After picking up a few pies from Tower of Pizza, they went to the bar for a staff meeting, then they turned the bar over to the boys to handle whatever drunks needed booze on the Lord's Day.

Seely knew she wasn't gonna see Seegar and she had an imaginary itch in the middle of her back from the sermon to the Lord's Prayer. The wooden pews didn't make it easier, but finally she just gave up, hunching over while kneeling.

That fidgety feeling returned during the meeting and she kept hopping up and down off the stool until Norton yelled at her to sit still. But she couldn't so she didn't and he finally called the meeting short, his patience exhausted.

Norton went into the back office and Seely set up the bar for later business when she felt a shadow cross her. She looked up to see the prominent teeth of Hildy beaming upon her.

"Hildy," Seely said, trying to pretend she didn't know what the goddamn Amazon was smiling about.

"Where y'at, girly?"

"I'm doing okay."

"Good. Cause you and me, we gotta look out for each other."

"We do?"

"Yeah. We're the daughters of powerful men. We may just run this little block one day. And I know if you have problems, I may be one of the few chicks who actually understands."

"Never thought about it that way."

"I hope you're with me."

"I am." Seely smiled and Hildy seemed to be finished. Tony's daughter went through the office door, emerging shortly with one of those omnipresent brown folders, probably just like the ones Norton used to collect before Mr. Black left for the North Shore and Norton bought the bar.

Seely, distracted, guessed that was Hildy's way of saying she approved of what she was doing. Hildy might even be helping. Seely didn't know if that was dangerous for her and Seegar or if Hildy was the one playing with fire.

Hildy hated doing any work on the weekend, but Tony only collected from Norton on Sundays. Some sort of deal the two set up years ago.

After talking to Seeley, she found Norton filling the folder.

"Hey, kid. I knew you'd be here soon."

"Yeah, I like to get this out of the way, then get back to the Goat."

"Girl, you worry that car to death. Just let it be."

Hildy shook her head as Norton gave her the folder. She snapped her fingers as she turned to head out. "Pop has a new guy aboard. He might be collecting soon."

"What new guy?"

"Name's Seeger. You might've seen him around."

Norton slammed his safe shut, then stood to look Hildy in the eye. "He don't come here. You come here."

"It ain't my call, Mr. Norton."

"Make it your call. I can tolerate him in the bar as long as my daughter don't give him free drinks, but he won't collect."

Hildy had never seen this side of Norton. Her father always said how cool he was in pressure situations, but here he was red in the face over some punk kid. "Okay. I'll collect. You've earned the right."

"Damn straight, I have."

Hildy ran out so she wouldn't get mad at the old man, blowing it for the two kids.

Soon, the illicit became the routine. In the first week, the newly-minted couple met every night, doing little but exploring each other's' bodies in a series of hotel rooms so they weren't rolling on the shag carpet floor of Seegar's apartment.

But as careful as they were not to be seen in the streets, they took too many chances in the dark. Seegar ran out of rubbers a few times and still they practiced their gymnastics, hoping for the perfect dismount without any problems. They were pretty sure they did it right.

But they couldn't run their scheme too often, as Norton might figure out his new sleeping habits weren't natural. So they picked off nights, Tuesdays or Wednesdays, so Norton wouldn't know why he was so tired.

Seegar slowly collected all the modern things that make a modern life. He drove this god-awful Thunderbird, an emerald green monstrosity that felt like driving a yacht. He got a queen-sized bed he mounted on a metal stand. Afterwards, they turned their sexual gymnastics to Seegar's place, showing a lot less fear.

But being young, they couldn't resist the siren's call of the nightlife, climbing in the T-bird and cruising to the French Quarter, a place as alien and mysterious as Mars, even if it was the most identifiable scene in New Orleans.

At first, they did the tourist's stroll, walking the pedestrian part of Bourbon Street, taking in the lurid photos outside seedy strip clubs. They looked up at the swinging legs over the transom of Big Daddy's strip club, peeked down back alleys at the entrance to the "French" live sex shows, never working up the courage to actually step in. They went into Pat O'Brien's for the tall and powerful drinks, rainbow-hued sweetness tweaking their libidos.

But they didn't pierce the hidden heart, until Seegar told Hildy what they had been doing.

"You ain't been to Lucky Pierre's yet?"

"I have no idea what you're talking about."

"It's this place in the Quarter. That's where some real freaky people hang out."

"And that's cool?"

"Seriously, you been hanging in Metairie for too long."

Hildy told him to meet her on Bourbon the next time they went out, giving Seegar the address. They planned for a Sunday, when Seely didn't have to work and there was a release from Norton without having to slip him the mickey.

Lucky Pierre's was not one of the bars that opened onto Bourbon, but was on the second floor above a tiny restaurant that charged twice the normal prices for below-average gumbos and jambalayas. Upstairs, a perma-cloud of smoke surrounded the amber lights, making the air grainy, the shadows clinging to the corners crawling along like haints. Bare tables, wooden floor, mahogany bar; everything in this place was old, like stepping into the 19th century. Seegar felt it must be haunted.

But the crowd impressed the young soldier. These men weren't wearing mall leisure suits and polyesters screaming at 40 decibels. These suits were linen and tailored, looking like second skins. And the women, whoa. Seely was as beautiful as any, but there was a precision to their fashion, a living tableaux of life in the '70s created by some Dutch master. These weren't rich people or middle class hustlers. No, these was the fabled bohemians and Seegar saw something he never saw in Fat City: relaxation.

These people weren't preening for attention. They laughed, nodded, sipped wine from heavy cut glasses and carried on from table to table. Their familiarity bred conviviality and both Seegar and Seely glided through the place with smiles on their faces. In the corner, Hildy waved them over.

Seegar had never seen this Hildy before. Wearing a dress, red halter top emphasizing her mid-sized but round breasts, lip shade complementing her clothes, and skin glistening like porcelain, she still had that horsey way about her, but now it seemed elegant.

"Damn, Hild." Seely gawked. "You ain't never like this around Macallister's."

"Thanks, Seely. I rarely feel the need. No offense."

Seegar pulled a chair out. "All those guys would probably laugh if they saw it."

Hildy popped Seegar's upper arm playfully, but he still felt the pain. "Shut up. They'd be all up in my face trying to get some of this and you know it."

"I feel underdressed now." Seely wrapped her arms around her chest. "It ain't just you, either."

Hildy pulled them close. "These girls, they look like this for a reason. Most all of them are working, if you know what I mean."

"No way!" Seely's eyes bugged.

"Yeah. Most of the men are named John. Or they're artists and these are their models."

Seegar's chin dropped to his chest and Seely spit through closed lips, which turned into giggling.

"Rubes. Both of ya." Hildy stood. A sharp-suited man walked into the bar, hair the color of tar and permed into a wavy pompadour like a TV newscaster. They slinked into each others arms and he bent Hildy back with a deep kiss. He moved with economy, scanning the room with his eyes only until he lowered into a seat.

Holding his hand out to the younger man, he said, "Name's Dino." Thick accent and deep voiced.

"Seegar. This is Seely." Dino kissed Seely's knuckles, then drew

Hildy close under his right arm.

"This is our young blood," Hildy said as she leaned into his embrace.

"Does he ..."

"Naw. But I guess he should. Dino works for Mr. Navia."

Seely seemed more surprised. "Really? Wow."

Hildy pointed at the blonde woman. "She's Norton's daughter."

"Good man. Good man." Dino nodded, but looked into the crook of Hildy's neck. He continued speaking, however. "You work at the bar?"

"Yeah."

"And you work for Tony?" He pointed at Seegar. "You work with brown paper products?"

"Yeah."

"We gotta start somewhere. I've been collecting papers myself for a long time."

"And that's the gig?"

Hildy sneered at him. "You bucking already?"

"Hell, no. Just getting my bearings for the long haul."

"Good. Now, relax and have fun here. We're gonna split."

"What?" The blonde youths spoke simultaneously.

"Easy. I'm opening a door. You're walking in and finding something new." Hildy whispered in Dino's ear and he waved while heading out the door. "We're like you. I don't want no strings and Dino's got a wife. We just have some fun and we don't have much time. So ..."

Hildy walked away, but stopped at a table where two forty-ish men were chatting. They stood, walking over to Seely and Seegar, Chesire grins on both faces.

"Ah, Hildy says you two are fresh meat from Metairie. We simply must talk. I'm George and this is Lyle."

George was thin with a trimmed beard, long hair wrapped in a stubby ponytail. Lyle was heavy and clean shaven. Lyle spoke up.

"Don't be afraid. We don't bite. Well, we don't bite straight people."

George and Lyle spun webs of stories through the night, talking of Tennessee Williams, Truman Capote, painters, fallen sons of carnival kings, randy daughters of politicians, the founding of

Preservation Hall and "characters, characters, characters," which Lyle bellowed after every anecdote.

They listened a little, wanting to hear of Metairie, mostly how tacky and bourgeois it was. An old lady brought a duck into the bar just after midnight, buying it two shots of bourbon. When it quacked loudly, George called out, "Ruthie, you know the duck's limit is one." Lyle cackled loudly at the *bon mot*, the rest of the table laughing at Lyle.

When they finally staggered out at three a.m., Seegar and Seely tried to remember half of what they'd been told. They made promises to return the following Saturday to meet the rest of the gang. Neither felt right driving back with so much liquor in their system, so they wandered down Bourbon to a small diner called The Clover Grill. They split an order of cheese fries, content that for at least a few hours they were in the right place.

Norton heard thumping in the early morning. He didn't rise, even though he was wide awake. He had been all night and still thought he might find some rest. It wouldn't come.

He boiled coffee, drinking two cups. If he wasn't going to sleep, he might as well be sharp.

He pushed open Seely's door, looking at her splayed out in a drunken stupor. He smiled, knowing he had done the same too many times. He knew what kind of pain was imminent for his daughter, but couldn't bear it for her. She'd have to go this one alone.

He got in the car, driving straight to Tony's garage. After he rang the bell, his old friend waited at the top of the stairs.

"This is a surprise. You ain't been 'round for a while."

"Bar's nuts. I put too much time in, but I'm getting a bunch out. Well, you know that."

"That I do."

They went into the office and sat.

"So."

"Yeah."

Tony put his good eye toward his old friend, seeming to see into his soul. "I ain't gonna like this, am I?"

Norton didn't say a word, putting a bottle of bitters on the desk.

"It's a bit too early for a snort. And I thought you ..."

"I did. But I've been real tired lately, like in the days when I took too much drink."

"I remember some of those nights. Others not so much."

"Right. Well, my stomach ain't right, so I have some soda water with a few dashes of this stuff to settle it. Some nights, I find myself on the couch in my office."

"And you don't know how you got there?"

"Yeah. So, I found a separate bottle of bitters two nights ago. And woke up on the couch after a few squirts."

"Who makes your drinks?"

"You know. And you know why she's doing it."

Tony knew Norton didn't want Seeger in Macallister's. He did the math, saying, "I can guess. Look, I've never seen you get this way before. I like this kid. A lot."

"Do you know why Judy left town?"

Tony found himself on the bottom of an aquarium. He could see Norton, but his vision was wavy and words didn't penetrate despite seeing lips moving. It didn't matter. He knew what Norton was saying and he had to do what Norton asked. "So what do I do about this?"

"Tony, I've asked you for many favors over the years."

"You've always earned it."

"This one you might not want to grant."

"You want to go that far with it? You ask me that?"

"He might be my blood, but he ain't my son like Seely is my daughter. They were drugging me, for God's sake."

"Why not just ..."

"That was a promise I made to a dead woman. He should never find out."

"You promised her that?"

"She made me swear. My mother's eyes."

"Jesus. Go do something. Get away. Let me think."

"I'll be at the bar."

"Alright. Shit." Tony slammed his fist on the top of the desk. This was not part of the bargain when he hired the kid.

Hildy came into the garage around ten, wearing those ridiculously huge sunglasses in his office like she was a goddamn Hollywood star.

"Take those fucking glasses off."

"What the fuck? I'm still ..."

"I don't care if you got pneumonia, I want those glasses off."

Hildy pulled them off, revealing the raccoon-eyes of a hangover. But she kept her mouth shut.

"Look, Seegar's fucked up. Hugely. Norton was in here earlier."

Hildy looked into her thighs. "What did he want?"

"Norton told Seely to stay away from our new prodigy. The two of them didn't listen. Then, they started slipping him mickey finn to keep him from knowing."

"Really? That is fucked up." Hildy tried her best to keep her tone neutral. Tony didn't sense anything wrong.

"Yeah. So Norton wants him dead."

Hildy jumped to her feet. "You didn't say yes?"

Tony waved her down. "Cool it. I didn't say anything."

"It's just two kids."

"It's still disrespect. Either way, the kid's out. I want him gone."

"Really?" Hildy's look pleaded with her father.

Tony stared at her. He hated having no depth perception, because his inner radar just went off but he couldn't plumb his daughter's lines.

"Get him in here. I'll give you two hours."   Hildy stood up and left. Tony picked up the phone. Norton picked up on the third ring. "You talk to Seely?"

"Yeah. She was throwing up. What the fuck did they do last night?"

"What we used to do before we got respectable."

"Yeah, right."

"Look, get over here now. It's going down."

Hildy beat on Seegar's door for five minutes. The young man answered the door in his underwear and she pushed past him.

"Get dressed"

"Shit, give me a sec."

"You don't have a sec, shithead. Norton knows."

That woke Seegar up. He threw on clothes while Hildy pulled out his duffel, stuffing wrinkled masses into the bag.

"This is not him coming to my office." Tony stood over them.

"Dad?" Thick-set wrinkles aged Hildy's face.

"Norton won't listen to me. Keep doing what you're doing." They finished with the bag. Seegar looked at Tony, but his face quickly pointed back to the floor. "I'm sorry to lose you, kid. But you don't do that shit. That said, I don't like Norton going rogue on me either." Tony pulled a .45 out of his back waistband. "Take this in case he tries to find you."

Seegar grabbed the gun, putting the bag over his shoulder. "I ..."

"Shut the fuck up and get out. I never see you again."

Hildy grabbed Seegar while she tried to hold back her tears, but a few strays puddled in the crooks of her eyes. As she let go, the front door slammed and Norton walked in, a .38 level to Seegar's chest.

Tony pushed Hildy up against the wall while Seegar aimed the automatic.

"You don't want to do this." Seegar pushed his chin out to rile up his courage.

"Boy, are you wrong, kid."

Norton cocked the gun. Seegar pulled his trigger three times. Three snaps, no firing.

The .38 flashed and Seegar crumpled.

"The gun was empty? What the fuck, dad? What the fuck?"

Tony slapped his daughter hard, shutting her up. He turned to Norton.

"Go. You got what you want." Norton ran out. Tony grabbed both of Hildy's hands with his huge right. "C'mon. You get in the car."

"What?"

"I'm taking you to Grand Coteau. You going into a nunnery."

"The fuck I am!"

"You talk like you got a choice." Hildy crumpled, but Tony pulled her down to the street.

Norton was covered in sweat when he got home. He jammed the a/c down to 65 degrees and sat on the sofa, trying to catch his breath. He was about to look in on Seely when she walked in the front door.

"Where did you go?"

Seely sat on a chair across from him. She was holding back a full-on bawl.

"Baby, I didn't want to, but ..."

"What?"

"I couldn't."

"Dad, shut up.   I just got back from the doctor. I'm two weeks late."

"Fuck!"

"I guess you can call yourself grandpa now."

The dams burst, Seely falling to her knees crying. She reached out for Norton, but he was shaking from his own breakdown and couldn't look at his daughter.

PART THREE: THE BERLIN WALL

Khaki shirt with two pockets and short sleeves. Khaki pants, thick from the military cut. Black shoes, military, to be shined once a week, encasing black socks. Never white. Ziggy had donned the uniform of Catholic school for a long time and he was sick of it.

Every day, he got on the two buses to go into New Orleans, to Mid City, to the Jesuit school. Then he would get back on the same buses, opposite direction, the purple-striped black bus marked Canal Cemeteries, then the blue bus named Veterans that took him back to Metairie, back to Fat City.

He knew he was marked, feeling the pointing and giggling of the girls who would only date Rummel boys. They would tease him, calling him a "Blue Gay" after the blue jay school mascot. Some of these cackling crows had gone to St. Angela Merici with him, but they didn't like him and he sure as hell didn't like them.

Soon, however, he knew they would be begging him to be their boyfriend. In a few days, he would turn fifteen and be able to drive.

But like everything in his miserable life, it all depended, specifically on that little troll Mimi who had somehow become his guardian. He still remembered the dark-suited men sliding his grandfather Norton into the yawning maw of the mausoleum when he was nine. The old man had been cool to him, mostly because he was drunk a lot. They would laugh and play until he passed out. He turned the bar over to managers who stole way more than they should have, but kept the place open. All Ziggy knew of his mom was faded Polaroids at the bottom of a drawer in his room. Norton never said anything about it, like Ziggy had just turned up one day. Ziggy was too young to care.

So Mimi took him in. She was Seely's best friend, or that's what Mimi told him. Compared to those pictures of the willowy blonde, Mimi was squat, thick and had a face like an Eskimo. Six years later, he was in the back apartment of a bar called Club Berlin that Mimi owned. And she kept the leash tight on her young charge for reasons the boy couldn't figure.

The place was more of a dance club, playing that electronic shit for weirdoes. It wasn't pop, like those New Kids records he listened to a few years back. No, the people who came into Berlin had blue-black hair and pasty skin. Looking for something to listen to, Ziggy combed the DJ booth, finding bands with names like New Order and The Banshees. It was 1992. Why wouldn't these people let the '80s die? Berlin didn't open until seven, so when Ziggy let himself in the front door, Mimi was wiping down the bar.

"Hey, kid." Her voice was like a knife dragging across brick.

"Hey."

"What kinda cake you want? I was thinking maybe doberge." She pronounced the name of the pudding-layered cake as "dough-bash" like most New Orleanians. "I could pass by Gambino's."

"Sure."

"You don't want dat, I could get something else."

"That's fine."

"Don't get too excited."

"Okay." As he walked to the apartment, he heard her say something else. "Never speak again," he thought as he slipped into his room. He turned on his stereo and pressed play on the CD player. He had listened to only one disc for the last three weeks and he would listen to it again right now.

The opening guitar riff chimed in, heavy and vicious and made boring ass life in boring ass Metairie disappear for a few minutes. He tried understanding what the singer was saying, but could only catch snatches of the mumbled lyrics. He knew he heard "here we are now, entertain us" rhymed with "stupid and outrageous," but the rest was a blur. He banged his head until "Smells Like Teen Spirit" came to an end, then sat down with his Religion textbook to do homework while listening to the rest of the album.

Mimi knocked on the door, signaling dinner was on the table.

It was Wednesday, so that meant meat sauce and spaghetti with a salad of iceberg lettuce and carrots.

They had a silent prayer before eating.

"You play that record too loud."

"It drowns out the club."

"We ain't open yet."

"I meant when you're open."

"Then why's it so loud now?"

"I don't know."

"I know. You think I didn't listen to Zeppelin like that, making Alvar mad at his little sis for making so much noise."

"Sure."

"You're just fifteen. At least in a couple days. Listen as loud as you can stand it."

"Gee, thanks."

Mimi looked at him with one eye closed. Ziggy knew she hated lip, but this time she let it pass. "So, Saturday?"

"Yeah?"

"You wanna get the license?"

"Definitely." Ziggy actually smiled. Mimi returned it.

"I remember wanting it so bad. I gotta let you do it."

"When can I take the car out?"

"It ain't gonna be your car, you know that?"

"I know." Ziggy deflated.

"But I want you to get out a little. You just lay around here all the time."

"Thanks."

"It's cool," she said, but Ziggy saw her plump with happiness.

Friday rolled away like a bead of sweat, the school day whipping by. Friday night was when Mimi picked up a large pie from Tower of Pizza. She had a couple of slices, then went into the bar, readying for the night ahead.

He ate and watched TV, laughing at Bob Saget and that kid who played Urkel, but the box finally held little interest for him. He turned it off, picking up his book of Greek mythology. He had read it many times, combing the intricacies of each story: Hercules conquering every labor, but did little as part of the Argonauts; Zeus changing into everything imaginable just to get laid without

Hera seeing it; and, of course, Icarus flying too close to the sun. These heroes and gods seemed like kids his age, lying and chasing tail and acting stupid. But it was fun for him to get away from his own thoughts and soon he was awake on Saturday morning.

Mimi always went to bed late, so Ziggy turned on the cartoons and waited. Cartoons turned into college football, and still Ziggy waited. He looked in the fridge for a Coke, finding the cooler devoid of cans, so he went to the bar to draft one out. Between the waitresses' brass rails, he saw a smudged mirror and a plastic straw and knew that Mimi would never get up in time, even though the DMV was only eight minutes away.

He tried not to get too mad because then he'd never get his goddamn license. So he went into the piercing sun to check the mail. He didn't believe it; there was a small package with his name inscribed.

Back in front of the football game, he opened up the manila folder. There was a letter from a lawyer and a large key for a bank box. The number and address of the bank were listed in the letter. At the end, he read the name Seely Norton.

"Mom," he thought, hating he had to wait until Monday to see what awaited.

He stayed away from Mimi for most of Sunday. Luckily, the Saints won that weekend, so Mimi was in a great mood. She promised to pick him up from school the next day to take him to get his license.

The DMV was a squat little trailer complex at the end of Veterans, sitting on the New Orleans side of the 17th Street Canal, the official line between Orleans and Jefferson Parish. The little bridge could have a checkpoint, Berlin style, because residents of both sides hated crossing it.

Mimi and Ziggy were coming from the New Orleans side, driving past the multi-storied houses of Fountainbleu, the street which connected Canal, the main road of downtown, and Vets. They couldn't have looked more different: Ziggy head to toe in the khaki uniform and Mimi in acid-washed jeans and a zippered white vinyl jacket, Ziggy upset she was dressed like an extra from some old Michael Jackson video. Times were changing, but she fought the tide.

"You ready for this?"

Ziggy steeled himself. "Lemme ask you something."

"Sure."

"Why did mom leave?"

"You can't ask me that." She turned into the parking lot. When she threw the car into park, she turned off the car, killing the blaring radio. "I'll tell you anything about your mom from when we were friends, but that's something you just shouldn't know. Now, let's get in line before they close."

Mimi fumbled with a plastic zip-lock bag as the line slowly snaked toward the front desk. She pulled official-looking papers into order, looking at the sign laying out exactly what they needed for the application. When they finally got to the head of the line, the older black clerk looked them over with owl-y glasses as Mimi pushed the papers across the desk, her width extending over both applicants.

"You're not his mom?" Ziggy saw the woman looking for reasons not to give him the test.

"Those are my guardian papers."

"Hold on a minute." She was holding out Ziggy's birth certificate. "How come there ain't no father listed here?"

"That's what I got." Mimi's chin receded into her neck. That damn secret always hanging like ripened grapes on the tallest branch.

"Loretta, come see." Another black woman, this one thin but just as old, sauntered over to the station. She had half-glasses, looking through them by tilting her head up. "Is this okay?"

Loretta took the birth certificate and checked out the numbers.

"That's real." Mimi blew out a breath. Loretta looked over at Ziggy who tried to shrink like Alice after drinking from the bottle. "It's okay, baby, we don't mean to make no fuss."

The heavier woman brought Ziggy to a line of desks. She gave him a test booklet, a Scantron sheet and a three sharpened number twos. Because he took driver's ed, Ziggy knew the answers to the increasingly obscure questions, like when was the road at its slickest and how much room you should give a car ahead of you on the highway. He skipped one question about speed limits, the only one he missed. Mimi gave him the keys to the Toyota and a burly, flat-topped cop got into the passenger seat.

Ziggy took the time to buckle the seat belt over his lap, something

Mimi never did. The cop nodded, then told him to take a right on Fountainbleau heading toward Vets. The street was split into two one-way lanes, so Ziggy looked to his left and turned right.

"You didn't look the other way." The cop's guttural voice scraped the tense air.

"It's one way."

"The drunk coming down the wrong way don't know that."

"Yes, sir."

They turned onto Vets, making their way past the parish line. Ziggy made a u-turn and headed back to the station, the cop chastising him again for not looking the wrong way up a one way street, that hypothetical drunk apparently careening around town looking for danger. They pulled into the parking lot and Ziggy got the third lecture on the multiple drunken wrong-way danger jockeys, but the cops signed off on his skills. They walked out of there with Ziggy's teenage mug shot laminated and paid for.

Mimi took the reigns for the drive home, but he got her to promise he could take the car to school the next day. He said it was so he could celebrate the rite of passage, a term culled from his mythology book. Mimi bought it, but his mind could only think of that safe deposit box.

School ended at 3:10 and by 3:30, Ziggy stood in a windowless room filled with locked slots of secrets. The man in the gray suit said he went to Jesuit too, pointing at the arm patch with the blue jay. Ziggy smiled, but didn't want any small talk. The guy asked if a few teachers from his time were still there. Two were and one wasn't. He finally got the hint, leaving Ziggy alone with the box sitting on a chest-high table.

Opening the black locker, he found a clear plastic case in the center, gleaming from the overhead fluorescents. It was a Super Bowl ring with the the Roman numeral one on it and he realized how valuable this thing was. There was also a small envelope that bulged at its left side. He pulled out papers, the bulge two keys on a ring, one obviously for a car.

One paper was a certificate of authenticity. The ring was real and belonged to Paul Hornung. Ziggy knew he was a Packer, but not much else. He read the other page, a letter signed by Seely.

"Ziggy, I write this knowing I will never see you. I have saved enough to go to Hawaii and, by now, have drowned on some beautiful beach so that I can join your father in whatever waits for us after this life is done. Norton, my father and your grandfather, stole his life because your father was also my half-brother."

Ziggy had to put the letter down. He rubbed his hands, looking at a normal set of fingers. He knew his body was solid and healthy. All of those stories of two-headed children or genetic freaks from incest were not true in him. Still, he felt the secret smash him across the face like Thor's hammer, staggering him. He had to sit and dropped on the tile floor.

He re-opened the letter.

"Never let Mimi know you have the ring. She was my best friend, but she was obsessed with it because it was stolen from her brother Alvar. She promised me she would love you when Dad died, but I know she will not let this go. Sell it when it is time to go to college and leave her and Fat City behind. Live the life I couldn't."

There was an address below her name and a postscript.

"Here is your other inheritance. You should have your diver's license by now. If you ever need help with Mimi, Alvar or a man named Tony, go to the nunnery at Grand Coteau. Ask for Hildy."

He drove the Toyota to the address. It was a small garage with a side door unlocked by the other key. He stepped in and turned on a light. A car, covered with a dull canvas tarp. Ziggy pulled it back to reveal a classic GTO. The key fit.

The engine was dry so he couldn't start it up, but there was a title in the passenger seat, his name the last one listed. One final gift from a desperate mother for a kid she'd never see.

"At least," Ziggy thought, "I can't say she never gave me anything."

Ziggy looked at his watch, it nearing five. The garage was only five minutes from the club, but Mimi would ask questions if he wasn't home pronto. He left the Goat where it stood, rushing back to the club.

Mimi was cutting lemons and limes behind the bar when he walked in. He said he had given a school buddy a ride home, kid lived in Kenner, and they played a video game.

"I dropped so many quarters down that Asteroid machine," Mimi said. "Time goes quick. Okay, I'll be there in a bit."

It was ten o'clock, but Ziggy couldn't sleep. He hated living with

Mimi, but lately she had softened up. He thought she looked like one of the monsters that the mythic heroes had to face, maybe something like Medusa in her cave. He pictured her round pinched mouth, ruddy complexion and black hair sculpted into two side claws superimposed on a hawk's body, an '80s harpy of death. Her brother Alvar was a dwarf and couldn't help what he looked like. But Mimi was ugly inside and out. Now that her own best friend, his mother, had said not to trust her, how could he appreciate her being nice without getting suspicious?

Ziggy put on jeans and wandered out the alley door to the front of the club, the insistent electronic beats muffled by the front door. The parking lot wasn't full, but there was a pale girl sitting on one of the concrete stoppers, talking to herself. She looked close to his age.

"You okay?" Ziggy expected to be brushed off immediately because she was pretty cute.

"No."

Ziggy stood there silently, waiting for a command to leave.

"That bitch at the bar, the owner? She took my ID and said I can't come back." Ziggy remained silent, but moved closer. "I mean, it's fake."

"Yeah, she hates that. She's seriously paranoid of cops."

"You know her?"

"She my ..."

"She's not your mom, is she?"

"No. My mom is dead. She's my guardian."

"Are you mad at what I just said?"

"No, she's a bitch."

"Yeah, well, my mom is too." Ziggy sniffed an approximation of a laugh and the girl smiled at him. "What's your name?"

"Ziggy."

"Like the cartoon?"

"Yeah. Never heard that one before."

She giggled. "Sorry."

"Forget it."

"I'm Raven."

"Like the poem?"

"Actually, yes. Nobody ever caught that before."

He looked at her. Her hair was deep black, a tinge of blue, heavy black mascara drawn into little horns along her eyelash line. Shirt and dress were also black, but her mid-calf boots were oxblood red.

"You don't have school tomorrow?"

"Sure I do. I just don't care. Plus, the 'rents think I'm in bed anyway. I only live a few blocks away. Fuck it, I guess I'll get some sleep."

"Can I walk with you? I can't right now."

"Can't what?"

"Sleep.

"Oh. Sure."

They traded the standard info. She went to Sacred Heart, the small Catholic girls' school uptown. She hated Fat City and couldn't wait to move to the Quarter. Or maybe New York. She didn't love Nirvana like he did, but she liked some new music.

"I like the dance stuff some, but I'm really into Nick Cave."

"Who?"

"Oh my God! He writes these crazy dark songs about murder and love and obsession. He's the whole reason I'm goth."

"What?"

"The look? You don't know."

Ziggy shrugged. They stopped in front of her house.

"So much to learn. I'll come by tomorrow and hopefully you can get my ID."

"Yeah. Like four?"

"Sure."

They stood apart for a fleeting moment and she spasmed.

"You okay?"

"I thought you were gonna try and kiss me."

"I wasn't."

"You should."

And so, he also spasmed forward, managing to find her lips. No arms, no embrace, but a taste of cherry. She pulled back and started up the walk.

"Oh, Ziggy? If you see me during the day, call me Mary Catherine. Raven only comes out at night."

He thought she was weird as he shambled back home. But he'd

accept that first kiss, weird or not.

Ziggy always got up alone. Mimi couldn't finish work before 4 a.m. and he had to be at school by 7:15. They would pass each other on Friday mornings because the college crowd made Berlin one of their last stops. She called this "the changing of the guard," as she sloshed into cotton pajamas and a waiting bed.

But she was long under this Thursday morning. He opened the door to the club, moving quickly just in case, finding one license sitting next to the register. It didn't say Mary Catherine and the older woman in the picture was way too close to 30 to be a teenager. And the name seemed fake: Hildegard Murano. He scooped it up anyway, then headed to the bus stop.

He spent most of the day trying to figure out how to get to the auto parts store, then score some gas to see if the car would start. The whole thing seemed out of his league, like if some high school pitcher was all of a sudden called up by the Yankees. While the car was legally his, he didn't want Mimi to know about it. Walking the tightrope of deferred pleasure had always been his specialty, so he could ride this out until all seemed right. Hopefully, it wouldn't take much time.

He decided to change out of his uniform before he went to the auto store, so he headed home from the bus stop. As he cracked open the bar's door, he heard voices inside.

"She even tried to use Hildy's license, like I wouldn't know who she was."

"I'm glad you told me." This voice was male, rumbly New Orleans accent, possibly Italian. "I don't want her out in bars until she's legal. And even then ... No disrespect."

"Look, I know you can protect me from the cops, but I don't want no law in here if it don't have to, you know?"

"Oh, yeah. You see her again, let her stay. But call me so I can catch her. Then you definitely will never ..."

The voice stopped abruptly. A column of light signaled Ziggy's arrival and he walked in. Mimi smiled, which only made Ziggy more nervous.

"Hey, Zig. I want you to meet Tony."

The man who held out his hand was chunky, but looked tough. He was smiling, which made the nylon patch over his left eye inch up to the point where it could reveal what was beneath. Ziggy remembered his name from the letter, shaking the hand limply and fighting off his flight instinct.

Mimi pulled a piece of paper out of her back pocket.

"Zig, I found this in the trash. Did you even read it?"

Ziggy took the paper from her, pretending like he wasn't screaming inside.

"Yeah. So?"

Tony stepped up to him. "Ziggy, your grandfather was one of my best friends. In fact, I was instrumental in clearing the way for Mimi to be your guardian because of his tragic death."

"Thanks." He half-smiled at Mimi who returned it with a beam.

"Did anything else come with this letter?"

"No. I figured it wasn't anything. I mean, you told me she left nothing behind but me."

Mimi started to speak, but Tony held up his hand. "It's not that she left nothing, because we all have fond memories. But there might be a few things that would help towards your future."

Mimi looked at Tony, who stopped. She leaned toward Ziggy.

"I think if we got what's missing, I could adopt you. Then we could really be a family. Wouldn't you like that?"

A wan trickle of teeth passed for a smile.

"See," Tony said. "I can tell he's been waiting to hear those words for years."

"Great! Tomorrow, I'll pick you up from school and we'll go to the bank and see what this is. I mean, c'mon! Your mom left you something? Aren't you excited?"

"Yeah," Ziggy said. "I guess I thought it was a scam or something."

"Hey, that's smart thinking," Tony said. "You gotta be aware of who's who and what's what. But Mimi and I know the truth and this here is legit."

Ziggy finally excused himself, promising he would be ready to go the bank the next day. He changed and packed his book bag with clothes, as tonight he would be gone.

The car started up. Ziggy anticipated the oil being low, so he poured in a couple of cans to even it out. The engine spit fire, rumbling through the streets like a dragon beneath him. He filled up, checked the tire pressure, then bought a map. Where the hell was Grand Coteau anyway?

Right between Lafayette and Opelousas, a small river town with five stop lights and a nearby plantation. The Academy of the Sacred Heart loomed large on the local geography.

It was a girls' high school, a smaller primary and middle school (called St. John Berchman's) and a shrine. But it was quiet, especially to this young man from the bustling party center of Fat City.

The school was locked tight with a side door where a small light burned and a white plastic doorbell hung on the sill. He sat on it for a few minutes, until a gray-haired woman with glasses and clutching a robe around her opened the door.

"Young man, what could you possibly want?" She talked with a brogue, either Irish or Scottish, Ziggy couldn't tell. His inside desperation came to the surface in the yelping of his voice.

"Is there a Hildy here? I've come all the way from New Orleans."

"Why would Sister Hildegard want to see you?"

"She knew my mother. My dead mother."

The old woman's pursed lips relaxed and she let him into a small room. "Wait here."

He sat on a wooden bench while she went through a self-locking door. That name. He knew where he had just read it and, when the door opened, he saw the face on that old driver's license.

"You got to be Ziggy. I've waited years to see you." She pulled him into a warm and loving hug. She let him go, an excited look flashing across her face. "Did you drive the Goat?"

She ran outside and he hurried to catch the door behind her.

She hugged the car's black top, grinning toothlessly with her eyes closed. "You been treating her good?"

"I just got it two days ago. This is the first time I've driven it."

"Keys." She held out her hand, flapping her fingers impatiently. "C'mon."

He handed them over and she got in the driver's side. She waited for him to sit in the passenger seat to start up. He turned to say something, but she put her finger over her lips.

"Needs a tune. You take her to a garage when you get home. I'll give you some cash." She put the car in gear and drove away from the school. "Kid, I ain't been laid in fifteen years. But this is pretty good. We go up on the interstate, I might just come."

Ziggy saw years melt off her face, closer to the picture he'd seen.

"Can I ask you a question?"

"I'm sure I'm gonna have to answer a bunch."

"Why would some girl named Mary Catherine have your old driver's license?"

She looked at him sideways. "Shit, that's your first question? Damn, didn't expect that." She rubbed the top of his head. "My kid sister's pretty cute, ain't she?"

"I guess."

"Yeah. How did you see that?"

"She tried to go to Club Berlin. Mimi took it away."

"How's she doing?"

"She's been real nice to me lately."

"So, you must have met my dad, then. Tony?"

"Yeah. Today."

"I know. I helped your mom write the note. You hungry? The sisters don't let me eat at McDonald's."

They pulled into the fast food restaurant, the only one in the little town. Hildy told Ziggy all of the stories while he ate.

"So, you can't give that ring to Mimi and you can't give the ring to my dad. I mean, if you feel nice about it, you can give it to Alvar. But these people have done horrible things because of that bauble. None of them deserve it."

"My mom wanted me to sell it to pay for my college."

"That's probably a good plan. But I see one hitch." Ziggy shrugged his shoulders. "You got more than two years before you can even think about college. Mimi and Dad ain't gonna accept that the ring is lost. They will get it from you, even if they don't act right."

"Then what do I do?"

The question hung between them in the greasy air. Hildy slurped the last of her vanilla milkshake through her warbling straw.

"We'll let you sleep, kid. There's an empty room at the convent. Just know that Sister Martha has already called my dad and you're probably in trouble."

"Great."

"Eh, they ain't gonna kill you."

"How do you know?"

"You still have a bit of power. They have no idea where the ring is. Plus, they don't kill without reason. Dad still has a bit of his soul left."

They left the restaurant and Hildy took him to a bare room with only a bed and a pillow. As Ziggy looked in the closet, she brought in a scratchy wool blanket. He spread it over the dorm-style single.

Hildy stood over him, a head taller than this kid. She reached with her right hand, pinching the bottom of his chin.

"Damn, if you don't look like both of them. I never really realized how much they looked alike until I saw your face."

She leaned over and kissed him on the forehead. Smoke shadowing her eyes, she pulled up on his chin, kissing him full on the mouth, and he tasted her muscular tongue still coated with vanilla.

And, just as quickly, she pulled back, drawing him to his knees.

"Kid, we have to pray." Sitting to Ziggy's right, she grabbed his right hand with her left and raised her right to the ceiling. "Lord, please forgive me for straying from the path. I find comfort in the blaze of your light and run from Satan's darkness. Please help this young man stay on the straight and narrow and not be tempted by this sad sinner. And give him the strength to be like righteous Lot who you allowed escape from wicked Sodom. We pray for your blessings. Amen."

"Amen."

Hildy stood, leaving Ziggy on his knees. She opened the door to the cell and turned back to him.

"It was the sin of Envy that drove Zed Black to want the ring. It was the sin of Pride that drove his brother Zelco to kill him. It's the sin of Greed which drives Mimi and Tony to exploit you. Ziggy, you were born from the sin of Lust. Evil surrounds you and we have to find a release. I hope God will inspire us tonight to find a way out."

The glowing light from the hall formed a halo around her darkened face. She had seen deep into his soul and Ziggy thrummed in her presence. As she closed the door, he felt the desire that only a fifteen-year-old boy's body can create.

His whole body felt erect. He stripped bare and jerked himself, feeling the soothing burn of orgasm. He wiped himself with his socks and fell deeply into slumber, the ride and the revelations and the sensuality all collapsing into a black hole of sleep.

He knew he was dreaming. He was taller, lean and wiry from battle. The sword dragged his belt to the left, held in place only by his sharp hip bone. He wore a short tunic and dry sandals while he trudged through a sandy-bottomed string of mountains. He was searching for something within the rocks and needed to find entrance.

He rounded a jutting crop of boulders packed with thin moss, finally seeing the cave. Hot air gurgled over him with the rumble of belabored breath and he unsheathed his sword just as the dragon's head emerged from the darkness.

"Zelco!" Ziggy heard himself shout the name. His conscious mind shuddered at the call. Like old Mr. Black? That Zelco? "I have come for you."

"I have waited, young warrior, for you to arrive. You who would stake his claim on my head. You who would dare take my heart from me and exhibit it to the world? You may have daring, but you are no match for my strength."

A clawed front foot bolted out, pounding him full on the chest, and he felt himself rising and flying back. But he knew to tuck himself tight, rolling as he hit the ground.

Zelco wriggled out, showing his full wyrm's body, snake-y red scales overlapping through a whip-like tale, legs and claws like a leather lion. The lizard head was mottled with calcified bumps and a hinged jaw held back a forked tongue.

"My heart fuels this world, whelp. There is nothing without my enshrining aura. Attack me and you attack the earth itself."

Zelco snapped at Ziggy. The boy-man dodged to the side, hearing the toothed vise crack like a gun shot. Ziggy jabbed at the dragon's face and the blade caught purchase just under the nostrils. Zelco's neck craned back, voice roaring.

Ziggy scrambled up the rock outcropping.

"You cannot escape me. But you should run, for I shall see you die this day."

Zelco followed him up the rocky path, body slithering up the stones, drawing quickly up to Ziggy. He darted his neck back to make one final strike, but Ziggy dropped the sword and hoisted up a boulder the size of two watermelons. As Zelco struck, Ziggy forced the huge stone into the dragon's mouth.

Zelco's neck recoiled and thrashed as he choked. Ziggy picked up the sword and darted under the dragon's maw. As the dragon snapped to the ground to free his breath, Ziggy thrust upward. The sword cut through the soft flesh of the under-jaw until Ziggy's arm was buried to the elbow. Scalding ichor covered his chest, but Ziggy surged through the killing blow.

He cut into the dead dragon's chest to reveal the bejeweled heart. Ziggy's eyes snapped open when he saw it looked exactly like the ring.

As Ziggy finished dressing, he heard a knock. Hildy walked in.

"Okay, brace yourself." Ziggy looked into her eyes. "I called my dad. He and Mimi are waiting for you at the club."

"What?"

"They think you're bringing them the ring."

"No fucking way."

"Exactly. You don't bring them shit. I got something up my sleeve and I'm not gonna let them get away with anything."

"And I should just trust you?"

"Who the hell else can you trust? By the way, old Zelco Black died last night. He'd been sick for years, but he's gone now. More wages of sin."

Ziggy fell into a reverie that didn't let up until he hit the Causeway exit on I-10.

When he got to Club Berlin, he heard shouting within. He snuck in the front door, trying not to disturb the fight. Tony held up an ice pick to Mimi's face.

"Do you fucking know what this fucking is?"

"Yeah, ice pick. Bars have ice picks."

"Real observant. Bitch, this is the pick that your brother used to take my eye out. Why is this here?"

"Alvar said to hold onto it. I don't ever use it."

"Well, I'm taking it and throwing it in the goddamn lake."

"More wages of sin?" Ziggy was surprised by the confidence in his voice. "Eye for an eye? Or should you turn the other cheek?"

They both calmed down as the saw Ziggy. Tony spoke first.

"Kid, this bitch and her dumb shit brother." He was laughing, but there was little mirth in his tone. "They always got me in the middle of things."

Mimi, ignoring the insult, walked over to Ziggy. "You brought us the ring?"

"Is that the only reason I'm even here?"

"No, Zig. I mean, I promised Seely. But she promised me the ring when you was old enough to be on your own. I mean, I done good by you, right?"

"My mom left me a note. It said the ring is mine and you two shouldn't have it."

Tony came closer now. "That ain't what Norton said."

"I guess she didn't listen to him. Again." Suddenly, Ziggy felt the prick end of the pick push into his lower jaw.

"I've lived without my eye for twenty years. I took that ring. Zelco's dead and now it's mine."

"Wait," Mimi's screeched. "Alvar won it fair and square. It's mine."

Tony forgot about Ziggy and screamed in Mimi's face. The little shrew yelled back, the bar echoing with cacophony. Ziggy backed slowly toward the door until he bumped into something.

He looked up. It was a man in a suit, who put a finger to his lips and motioned that Ziggy should put his fingers in his ears. As he did, the man raised a .45 and shot the bottles behind the bar.

Both arguers snapped their heads to attention.

"Dino?" Tony squinted at the new man.

"Tony. You ain't getting the ring."

"What?"

"Neither is she. Drop the shiv."

There was a clatter as the pick hit the tiled floor.

"The fuck is this?"

"Got a call from an old love this morning. I didn't forget Hildy."

"You and her?"

Mimi scoffed. "Everybody knew but you, dickhead."

"Shut up. It was a little fling for her and me, but I feel I still owe her."

"Mr. Navia ain't gonna like you working in my territory."

"Wrong. We had a talk this morning. We been letting you slide for a while, even though your crew is down to nothing and you ain't the big tiger you used to be."

"Fuck you, Dino. This ain't right."

"You can cry all you want, but it's over. As of today, you work for me."

Tony dropped down, scooping up the pick. Dino fired too late, the bullet breaking the mirror on the back wall. But Tony wasn't quick enough when he stabbed at Dino.

He shuffled to Tony's blind side, grabbed Tony's outstretched wrist. Twisting and pulling back, Dino hammered the gun on Tony's taught elbow, bending it the wrong way. A sickening crack brought Tony to his knees, tears filling the right side of his face. The pick fell out of his hand.

Mimi didn't hesitate. She threw Ziggy to the ground before he knew it, pouncing like a vicious cat and clawing at his face and neck with her long fingernails.

"I didn't do this for nothing. You gotta gimme the damn ring. I'll kill you!"

Ziggy flailed around, somehow the ice pick ending up in his hand. He had no idea what he was doing, but, like a marionette's string jerked, he felt his right arm stiffen, the point piercing Mimi's throat. He felt the metal snap out of the wood when she collapsed backwards.

Dino stood over Ziggy. He handed the boy a bar towel and Ziggy cleaned the blood from his face. Tony lay fetal as Ziggy stood up.

"You're safe now. I'm gonna take him to our doc, but I think you better skip town. This might take some time to blow over."

Ziggy threw his remaining clothes into suitcases. He would stop by the bank and drive the ring to Hildy. She would take care of it.

He saw Hildy's license in his wallet. He took the time to write a letter to Raven, not Mary Catherine.

"Your dad will hate me forever. Your sister saved my life. But I have to disappear for a long time. I may never see you again, but that kiss was one of the greatest things that ever happened to me. Hope you don't forget it either."

God, was that a lie. Hildy's kiss had been the one to move him. But he wanted someone closer to his own age to remember him. He had lived as a ghost behind the walls of Club Berlin. Now that

this life was over, he was burying a jewel to be dug up later.
Sometime when he could come back to Fat City.

PART FOUR: THE GODDAMN TWILIGHT

"Those are not drum sticks, pal. When you pick them up, ready to play, they become the hammers of the gods. Do you fucking hear me? You should sound like Thor driving a goddamn war party across the frozen tundra to kill and rape and plunder in burning rage. You keep playing like you're at a goddamn second line, like you're in the Neville Brothers or some shit, I will send your ass home."

Billy, the drummer, eyes both recessed and buggy, sagged on his throne. He looked small now, a smurf with a mullet. He pulled his sticks to his emaciated chest.

"Billy, the name of the goddamn club is Zepplin's. It's not Tipitina's, it's not The Maple Leaf and it sure as hell ain't no goddamn Muddy Waters or Howlin' Wolf."

The guitar player, blond locks cascading over his eyes, grumbled.

"What was that? Speak the fuck up, Jimmy."

Jimmy talked in that eighteen-year-old way: every statement a question.

"I was just saying about Robert Plant? How he dug the blues? Like 'When The Levee Breaks' is actually Memphis Minnie? And, like, Robert Johnson and Howlin' Wolf really wrote 'The Lemon Song?'"

"Thank you for that wonderful dissertation, Jimmy. You're right. But when you see kids showing up to this club, the club I own, they don't give a shit what old black farmhand wrote what fucking song. They want to bang their heads and they want to do it to speed metal. They want to pretend that you're as good as Jimmy Page or

Kirk Hammett or even Randy may he rest in peace Rhodes. But even that doesn't matter, Jimmy. Even if you were as good as those legends, which you certainly are not, what they really show up for is me."

Cobalt-shaded eyes peered over an outstretched arm and finger that swooped across the full bandstand, pointing at not only Billy and Jimmy, but Blake the bass player also.

"The name of this band is Valkyrie and I am the goddess our audience worships. I am the raven angel of the night that every swinging dick wants to lay into and every low self-esteem girl wants to be. I am the show, boys, and if you don't play like I want it, you will be replaced. Now, please."

And with this, the mouth turned from snarl to smile.

"I love you all and I just want us to be the best metal band in this town. So, let's do 'Crazy Town' the right way and one day we will all be stars."

Billy clicked his sticks four times, finally playing the snare correctly, like a war drum instead of a delicate piece of glass. Jimmy's fingers snaked along his guitar, ripping through the arpeggios in that dexterous metal way that guitarists have been doing for many years, at least since Eddie Van Halen changed the game. And Blake, well, he could play quarter notes fast enough to keep up with Billy. He would probably have to go when the record deal was signed, whenever that glorious day came.

Then Kate turned her back on these boys only recently shaking off the terrible effects of puberty and raised her voice to the non-existent crowd, spreading her arms over her head as she just missed reaching the high note.

"Crazy Town" was a weak rip-off of the similarly named Ozzie song, but the Fat City crowd didn't care. Anything that sounded like the old gods made them happy. They had stuck with Valkyrie through the fifteen different lineup changes, each with an announcement by Kate that soon she would get a record deal. She was still young and hot enough that everyone believed her, even though she only ever played at Zeppelin's, mostly because her dad owned the place and didn't care as long as the cops didn't come around.

But Kate believed. Because she stood tall in those six-inch

platform boots   Because she ruled over her queendom with benevolence. If you believed in Kate, she would smile upon you. The unbelievers, the haters, the worms were soon banished. And she ruled the place alone, for she had not yet met the man worthy enough to take his place by her side.

The song rumbled to its correct ending and Kate turned around, no longer in a whip-cracking mood.

"Now that, boys, was metal. Let's take a break. Blake, will you please go across the street and get our dinner." Blake put his bass on the stand and went out the glass door. "Jimmy, be on the lookout for another bass player. We can't let important people hear that shit. I'm going home for a sec. Call me when he gets back." She shook her cell phone at the guitar player, following Blake out.

It was six in the afternoon, but the summer sun glowered in the hazy sky. Kate pulled on her wrap-around Oakleys, feeling her hair wilt in the damp heat. It was only two blocks from the club to her house, but her forehead beaded to a glistening glow.

She wiped the sweat away with her hand, rubbing them on her black jeans. Some blond guy stood in front of her house, looking towards the door. She couldn't catch sight of his face, hoping it wasn't one of Dino's guys making sure the old man paid off his vigorish. But they were Italian, not tall and Viking like this one. And God, was he hot.

"If you're looking for Tony, today's the day he goes fishing. You're supposed to get the cash on Thursday."

He stiffened at the sound of her voice, but didn't look over at her. "Yeah?"

"Yeah."

"And what if I'm looking for Mary Catherine?"

It was her turn to freeze. She had made it perfectly clear when she turned eighteen that her name was now Kate. That old one screamed Catholic school girl, not rock goddess.

"Or at least I'm looking for Mary Catherine until the sun goes down. Then, I'm looking for Raven."

He turned and she knew exactly who he was. All of her posturing, all of her preening and all of her composure melted in a puddle on the sidewalk and she ran up to Ziggy, kissing him full on the mouth, like the scene at the end of the movie. The scene she had dreamed about for seven solid years.

He returned her passion, lifting the petite young woman until she wrapped her legs around his waist.

"You really came back."

"I said I would."

"Fuck, I didn't believe that."

"Sometimes I didn't either. But here I am."

They kissed again, then he lowered her to the ground. Her phone rang and she flipped it open.

"Hey. Y'all eat and go home. Yeah, something just came up. I'll let you know, but we are playing tomorrow. Yeah. Okay."

She grabbed his hand, pulling Ziggy away from her house. "My dad does not want to see you."

"I thought he was fishing."

"Shit, he never leaves the house. That's just the standard line."

"Dino still on his case?"

"Yeah. Come on, take me to dinner and tell me your lies."

She was happy when she saw the Goat. He said he wanted fried seafood, the one thing he could never get, so they drove down Vets to Fury's, a squat restaurant with ten glass-over-cloth tables and brimming with cold conditioned air..

They ordered the seafood platter, Ziggy pulling over the butter and crackers set out as a de facto appetizer. As he crunched down on a saltine, he said he had been waiting for this for years. That was lie number one. What he'd been waiting for happened last night. Tonight was lagniappe.

He had pulled into the convent's parking lot at dusk after four days crawling through Texas, even though the trip from Los Angeles should only take three. He didn't want to push the car past its breaking point, so he stayed below 55 on the interstate and kept a day's journey under 350 miles.

He had called ahead to tell Hildy that he'd decided to return to New Orleans. He first thought that maybe he should surprise her, but one of those nuns might not let him in this time. She laughed that bray of hers when he said who it was, her excitement crackling across the lines.

He rang the bell at the back door, Hildy coming down cloaked in a habit without the head piece. The formless black gown hung over her body like a popped balloon, but her radiating smile warmed him.

"Please, get me away from these penguins."

They drove into Opelousas, ending up on Main Street.

"Soileau's," she said. "That's the place to go."

Ziggy looked over the menu, food he hadn't seen the whole time he was away. He avoided all those West Coast places claiming to be Cajun or New Orleans. The memory was just too sharp. But now, catfish with a shrimp sauce sounded right on.

"They don't have food like this in L.A."

"Dino set you up alright?"

"Yeah. I split my time between L.A. and Vegas, just taking care of whatever Mr. Rourke wanted me to do."

"So, now you're part of a family."

"Close enough. I tell you what, though. Your reputation as a real badass made it all the way to the end of I-10."

"As it should have."

Even though he couldn't see her body, her face showed a leaner Hildy, tempered and hardened. Her hair with wisps of gray and eyes crinkling when she laughed, she had become something wizened. Gone was the stallion of youth, replaced by a warhorse.

"So, did they ever make you take the vows?"

"They did." She stared into her gumbo, her bitten lip a chink in her chain armor.

"You shouldn't have, right?"

"If you say something out loud, does it mean you believe it? Kid, I sat in that church and promised to become one of them. But, and this was obviously after you left, I didn't … I couldn't believe it anymore." He reached for her hand and she gripped his firmly. "They may call me sister, but it don't mean shit. I guess it never did."

His thumb probed her knuckles, caressing the ridges.

"Finish eating," she said, pulling her hand back to herself.

He told her about the West Coast, how things worked differently in an open mob town. He had learned to handle a gun, took some martial arts to hone his body. He had found himself in bad situations and came out untouched. Mr. Rourke didn't want him to leave.

"So, I guess I can't go back there."

"Not that you'd want to."

"Not at all."

He paid the tab and found her leaning against the car.

"Do you really have to wear that thing everywhere?"

"They want me to."

"But what do you want?"

She pulled at the front snaps, peeling away the frock. Underneath were a white t-shirt, jeans and motorcycle boots.

"I want to feel like I did so many years ago. Keys." He dropped the set into her outstretched palm. "Zig, do you know what not having sex throughout your thirties does to you?"

"Well ..."

"Shut up. It makes you mean and it makes you crazy. Frustration builds up in you and you just want to beat the crap out of any little boy who doesn't know his place. Do you know your place?" She grabbed him by his t-shirt collar, pulling him close. "Well, you're gonna find out."

She kissed him there, biting on his bottom lip until he tasted iron. They were soon at a hotel near one of the interstate exits.

He had lovers in Los Angeles, women eager to break him in and bathe in his fire. But they were acting, even those who weren't trying to be a movie star. They had watched porn, studying tape to see what kind of sex a man wanted. But to Ziggy it felt like a performance, something to applaud, not something to take to heart.

Hildy wasn't acting. She burst upon him, a flood of passion dammed up too long. Her lean body enveloped his hard muscles, squeezing with fury and leaving him breathless. She ground down upon him, pumping so fast he felt pain overwhelm him. But his young body could take the punishment and he leaned into her, pulling her body parallel to his own. They writhed together, her on top, the undulations synching until she gasped, groaned, then yelled an exhalation, finally crumpling in pleasure.

She dismounted, locking her lips around his hardness. The swirling tongue and the pivoting mouth made Ziggy feel caught in a whirlpool of ecstasy. His already brimming cock exploded in under a minute, but Hildy didn't pull back. She swallowed every ounce until he was flat.

She turned around and drove her ass crack onto his withering meat.

"Yeah, you've never had anything that good."

He laughed and she did the same and they lay bound together until she had to get back.

"So, you want the ring back?"

He looked out on the road back to the convent.

"Naw. I want you to hold onto it until I decide what to do with it."

"So that's still up in the air?"

"Yep. It's right next to what I'm gonna do when I grow up."

"And you're gonna grow up in Fat City?"

"That's the question, ain't it?"

He pulled into the parking lot and saw her tear up. She pulled him close and kissed him.

"Zig, I'm just a lonely old broad. Don't do something stupid with me if it ain't right."

"That wasn't stupid."

"No, it was great. But ..."

"Shut up. Don't give up on me yet."

She walked away, disappearing into the convent.

That last flash of Hildy reflected in the smiling face of Kate as she pulled the legs off a fried softshell crab. They looked enough alike, but Kate was not the racehorse her half-sister was. No, indeed. This one was a show pony. Even coming out of an afternoon practice, she was fully made up, maybe not what she wore on stage and certainly not the Egyptian queen who was once called Raven, but this face pined for a spotlight and he knew that anything he did to get between her and its luminescence would be bad news. He picked up a fried shrimp, running it through some tartar.

"When does your band play next?"

"Tomorrow. You gonna come by?"

"Wouldn't miss it."

"There is one catch. Zeppelin's, my place? It used to be Club Berlin."

It used to be my house, he thought. That's what she really meant.

"You clean that shit hole out?"

She looked disappointed. "Nobody lives there anymore, if that's what you mean."

A never-ending dance, he thought. Did he have the stamina for this? "I'm sure you've made the place special."

She smiled. "Yeah, it's way cool."

"What kind of music do you play?"

"Metal. Old school."

"No goth? Or grunge?"

"Naw. That's high school stuff. No moping, only rocking."

"Can't wait. I do have one problem." She looked up, eyes expectant. "No place to stay."

"You want your old room back?"

"I thought you said it was cleared out."

"So you sleep with boxes of beer and liquor. You can't handle that?"

"Is Tony gonna know?"

"His name may be on the papers, but he hasn't walked out our front door in three years. I don't even know if he could fit." Ziggy cocked his head. "He's put on about 70 pounds. Can barely walk."

"Sounds rough."

She shrugged. "It's hard to think a fifteen-year-old broke him, but that's what happened."

"That wasn't what I wanted."

"Can't change it. That's why my focus is the band. I stay away from the family business."

"Good."

She ran her index finger down the bridge of his nose, then gently grabbed the back of his neck, pulling him close. Her kiss tasted like fish, but he didn't care. She was beautiful and she was here now, not locked up with God's brides out in the country.

After dinner, it was only eight o'clock, so they drove to Wal-Mart and bought a sleeping bag and a pillow. Ziggy sprang for some foam padding, too, because Kate said the floor was slab. She had taken the carpet out to make it easier to cart stuff around.

While they drove back to the club, Kate drew into herself.

"Is it too early to ask what you're gonna do?"

"I know what I ain't gonna do. I ain't going back to L.A."

She frowned. "I need to go there, don't you think? They don't sign metal bands out of New Orleans. Hell, it seems like they don't sign anyone out of here these days."

"They say Napster's gonna change everything. You just need to put your songs on there."

"I can't record. I mean, I do well enough to live and keep the bar open. But even a demo is beyond my means right now."

"You can't save?"

"Did Mimi ever save?" Ziggy winced, not hearing that name for seven years. Kate must have had no clue about his last days in Berlin. "The margin is tight on a bar. I should put together a dope deal."

"I thought you stayed away from that."

"I do." She blinked at him and he stole a quick glance. "I do. Just, like, you get to thinking."

"Let me do some thinking. I have fresh eyes on this one."

She pressed her lips to his cheek. When she sat back, she curled her lip. "I do have a few bucks."

"Why do you say that?"

"Because I don't want to fuck you on my floor."

Ziggy lay back on the perfumey sheets of the hotel room. They smelled like aftershave on top of second hand smoke. He stared at the ceiling as Kate clung to him, naked and asleep.

Kate fucked like an actress. He felt like he was watching her in the footlights instead of bonding souls. She moaned and preened while grinding on top of him, he there to watch and come on cue. It felt scripted and he felt empty, especially after Hildy had ravaged him the night before.

In fact, Hildy was all he could think about. How could he rearrange her life to line up with his. Yeah, she was twenty years older, but her soul pushed out to her skin. She made life look like a horizon, not a brick wall. Eventually, sleep found him.

He jumped up the next morning to the sound of a shower. He lifted his naked self out of the stiff sheets and snuck to the bathroom. Kate was in the shower stall, pebbled glass only revealing her outline. He rapped softly on the door, her silhouette turning. The water stopped and the door opened.

Kate stood soaked before him. Her feet flat on the floor, he could now see how small she was, her poofs of poodle hair falling about her shoulders and across her forehead in dark curtains. Her face cleaned of make-up revealed the girl behind the goddess. Her smile was toothless and her eyes dipped. Ziggy saw he could love this creature, but knew a moment like this would never last.

"How about a towel, asshole?"

Spell broken, he engulfed her in bumpy cotton.

Ziggy spent the rest of the day in the back of the bar, dumbfounded that his childhood home was completely wiped away. Rootless his whole life, no father, his real mother gone and Mimi long dead, he saw Mimi's face as she watched afternoon soap operas on a crummy television, coffee cup on her pooch belly, cigarette dangling from her hand extending over the sofa, aloof and dead-eyed like Bellocq's Storyville whores. And like those women, she was just waiting for night to come so she could make a few bucks off common vices.

Ziggy moved a few boxes and set up a sleeping area in the corner, the modicum of privacy from the stacked cases offering no comfort. He took advantage of the alone time to slip into an afternoon nap. Kate had to spend the day with Tony and Ziggy was still tired from her pomp and circumstance the night before.

As he shifted onto his right side, he figured out his plan. He would spend the weekend here, milking some sweetness out of Kate. On Monday, he would head into the city to look for an apartment. He knew if he found a place in the Quarter or the Marigny, he would effectively disappear from Fat City. He would move Hildy in and they could live out their lives obscured by the suburban fear instilled in all who dwell in Jefferson Parish. When every puzzle piece fit, he dropped off.

He awoke gasping. Ever since having the dragon-slaying dream, his nights were roiling pits of despair. While he could never remember a dream, he greeted wakefulness as deep relief from the abyss. Kate was there, looking shocked.

"Are you okay?"

"Yeah. Sleep ain't exactly relaxing for me."

She kissed him on the cheek. "You should get up. The place will be open soon."

"Yeah?"

"Yeah. And I've lined up a surprise for you during the show tonight."

Ziggy smiled and Kate backed out the door, one finger over her lips. He shook his head at the little drama queen. So far, the show had been pretty good.

He walked into the bathroom, ran some water through his hair. He smoothed on some deodorant, changed into his club clothes and walked out to the bar. Three young guys sat on the stage, staring at him.

He ambled over. "You guys in the band?"

They all nodded. Each of them was not only young, they were super skinny. They didn't have the '80s poofiness Kate wore like a crown. Their long hair fell either dead straight or slightly curly, but always over their collars. One, behind the drums, had a picture perfect mullet and wore leather pants. The blond one, feminine face accented by eyeliner, pointed to him.

"You're the guy?"

"Say what?"

"Kate said some guy was staying here."

"Oh, yeah. Guilty. I used to live here."

"You lived in a bar?" The bass player looked surprised.

"Back used to be an apartment. When it was Club Berlin." Blank stares. "This was seven years ago when this was a goth dance club."

"Dude, we were, like, nine?" The blond one giggled at the thought. Ziggy willed himself not to feel old.

"Yeah, well, that's where Kate and I met. I took her home and kissed her and ..."

Their dropping jaws almost made Ziggy's ears ring.

"You kissed Kate?" The bass player ran a hand through his hair.

"C'mon. She's must've been through plenty of guys."

"Dude, you don't understand?" The blonde guitarist chopped with his right hand. "Kate is like a marble statue in a museum?"

"Or a church," the drummer dropped in.

"You look from far away? You relish the beauty and you maybe even worship it?" He then got real serious, his questions over with. "But you do not touch. You do not profane perfection with mere fingerprints."

Ziggy looked down his nose at the guitarist, the smoky reverie in his eyes showing no lick of sarcasm.

"You go to Jesuit, man?" The guitarist nodded. "Yeah, me too. Going to an all-boy school makes you say weird shit like that."

He pointed at the others. Drummer said Rummel while the bassist said Riverdale, the only public school kid. Ziggy hated himself for judging them, but he also felt he had these three figured out.

"Guys, I hate to break the news to you, but she's just a woman. No matter how many shots of Kool-Aid she hands out, no matter who drinks it, she's human. Fallible. Earth-bound. I would reserve my worship if I were you."

The bass player laughed mirthlessly. "Never say that to her, dude. Not if you like your balls attached to your body."

They picked up their instruments, making practicing motions. Ziggy decided now was a good time for a walk.

Lakeside Mall had changed so much. All of the movie theaters were gone and Maison Blanche had been taken over by Dillard's. He gave a passing nod to his old memories as he ate a burger at the food court. He never thought Fat City would change at all, but the place was rotting out around him, the film of decay hanging over that side of Severn, a patina of lost glory, the sad soot of neglect. He wondered if this place was ever new or shiny. The '70s maybe? When his mom walked these streets?

Kate waited for him behind the bar when he walked back in, her smile coy.

"You got my surprise?" She nodded, her lips pursed. She held out her hand and a little pill sat there. "What's that?"

"Ecstasy."

"The drug?"

"Yup."

"Wow." He had dropped a few times, but it had never done much to him.

"Tonight, when I take the stage, you take the hit. I'll do it right as we begin the first song. We should peak right at the climax of the set."

"You sure about this?"

"Oh yeah," she said. "I don't have a doubt in my head."

She walked to the side of the stage. He pulled back to the bar, the bartender instructed to give him anything he wanted on the house.

"Well?" The guy was another in a long line of Metairie metal heads, long hair rolling down his shoulders. Nowadays, in these few remaining years of the millennium, the goatee was required as the thin, fuzzy mustache just wasn't tough enough.

"Bottled water."

"Really?"

Ziggy nodded and the guy handed over the blue-labeled Kentwood. He walked to the front of the stage pretending to cough, but really slipped the pill into his mouth. He glugged a long drink of water, settling into a spot behind a group of younger women, hair length longer than their dresses.

Kate strode to the front of the stage, thigh-high boots sporting four-inch heels. She had fully transformed into a metal goddess, but Ziggy knew she was a decade too late. This look, this attitude, this whole fucking scene attempted to resuscitate a corpse. You could beat on the chest of glam metal all you want, but you'll never restart the heart. Yeah, maybe Motley Crüe and Ratt and Poison were still on the radio, but they had slipped into a Paleolithic time, captured in amber alongside Hendrix, Zeppelin and The Doors. Maybe this was the drug kicking in early, but all of a sudden Kate looked like one of those Mexican women he had seen on the Day of the Dead, a skull-faced version of rock and roll.

A wave of disgust passed over him.

"I'll be gone soon," he thought. "She can stay here and be queen of the graveyard. Don't bother me none."

Billy clicked his sticks four times and the band busted out a vintage metal riff. He saw Kate look at him and take a big swig from a light beer bottle. She winked, then stepped up to the mic.

They were playing "You Got Another Thing Coming" by Judas Priest, a poor choice from a purely aesthetic viewpoint. First of all, the original band had two guitars instead of one. The assault Jimmy laid down on guitar was thick, but couldn't cover the lack of depth. Secondly, Rob Halford was one of the great voices of '80s British metal, his vocal training letting him soar to the higher parts of the song effortlessly. Kate had raw talent, but Ziggy could tell she didn't have those kinds of chops. Her voice sounded thin, reedy even, the higher it went. Her muscle was down the scale, so trying to compete with the Priest made the whole band fall flat.

Not that the audience gave a shit. They were just happy that someone played this song live instead of hearing it through the dull speakers of a jukebox. The intense waves of live music played loudly made them rejoice at their goddess' feet, even if she wasn't all-powerful.

The band brought the song to the finish sharply. If anything, they were well-rehearsed. The crowd of twenty yelled, lifting their arms as if this cloister of a club were an arena and this band were bathed in light and fog.

As they went into the second song, Kate said into the mic, "This is one of our originals." For a second, she doubled over, almost fainting, but righted herself. Ziggy felt his own legs nearly give way, a nauseous flow beginning at the tips of his toes washed all the way up to his throat. But he didn't vomit, oh no. When he regained his balance, he was rolling hard, fully vested in the X. He could see Kate was also, pawing at her body and bursting with pleasure.

This song was "Crazy Town," and Ziggy saw it as the rip-off it was. But there was something else there. In a lower key than the Priest song, Kate was in her wheelhouse, singing with pure fire, but Ziggy also heard the lyrics, starting to see something other than an average bar band going through motions taught them by MTV.

"Caught in trap, a world I didn't make

"Nowhere to move as I shimmy and shake

"Where is the light that comes from above

"Feel like I can fly high as a dove.

"Someday I'm gonna get out of the crazy town."

Awful and cliché-ridden. Artless and pedestrian. But these words, combined with the halo of back lighting and a blood stream pumping pure endorphins, made Ziggy finally see her as a rose growing in the trash heap of Fat City. But she would die here, bitter and dreams unfulfilled just like her dad and half-sister, both trapped in prisons of their own making. In that moment, all of his love for Hildy drained, refilled by a welling passion for Kate.

As the song moved into the guitar solo, Ziggy looked into her eyes and spread his arms. Kate dropped the microphone and jumped down off the stage, strutting toward him as the people parted. She grasped him under his arms and he wound down upon her. Her height, increased by the boots, brought her just under his nose, the perfect level for him to bend and kiss her. This was it, a kiss even better than Hildy's all those years ago. This was the life he wanted to lead, Kate and him rejoined, prepared to conquer the future.

There were gasps audible over the thunder of the band. The girls squee'd as their heroine embraced romance with the handsome stranger, and the boys shocked that this guy, who they didn't even know, claimed the untouchable and unreachable woman. But the jealousy withered as they saw Kate's mask crack and fall, replaced by an unironic smile. He had changed her; the crowed saw that immediately. But none could see the tectonic shift happening within Ziggy, just that he was now their god in joint rule over Fat City.

Kate returned to the stage. Ziggy moved to the front row, letting all his nagging doubts about their talent disappear. Fully invested in the band's music, bouncing and banging his head, he was brought a stream of beers and shots of Jagermeister as if this gig was his and Kate's wedding reception. He was slapped on the back by the bros and the girls touched his arm while looking back and forth to Kate. His ascension had been quick, but he indulged the pleasure while the drugs kept him aloft.

After the gig, everyone wanted to talk to him. He told them the story of meeting Kate at 15 and having to leave town. He kept the details hidden, but it didn't matter if his story held up. They accepted him.

Finally, they all left and he was alone with Kate. He wasn't sleepy, even though the sun was starting to peek over houses. They decided to go get something to eat, walking over to a diner on Severn. After they ordered, Ziggy decided to get serious.

"How attached are you to the band?"

"The bass player has to go, but the other two are pretty good."

"So, it wouldn't kill you to find something better."

"No."

"Kate, Los Angeles is where the great players are. Also the record labels. It's where you need to be."

"I know. But Dad needs me and I have the club."

"You've used those excuses too long. I think you're afraid."

Kate pulled back from him, mask on the verge of reforming. "I ain't afraid of anything."

"You say that. But that's not the truth."

He saw she wanted to be strong, to be the Kate on stage and tell him to fuck off back to Los Angeles if he loved it so much. But, using his face as a mirror, she took a deep look within him. He could see what she was thinking: what did it matter if you were the fairest in the land if the land was a backwater swamp that kept your dreams unreachable?

"Tell me this. What will it matter if we move there? How could I possibly have a chance?"

"I did some of the same things your dad used to do." He knew she didn't like it, but she let him go on. "Those things had many fingers in many pies. One of the pies was the music business."

"So, you may know people?"

"I know people. But that's no guarantee."

"What kind of hope is that?"

"I've got a little cash, but I also have the ring."

Kate's eyes bugged. "You have the ring?"

"I have it safe. We can sell it, make a demo for you and then have enough cash to wait out the record business. Do you like the plan?"

"Yeah. I do. If you do."

"I have nothing in this world but that ring. But if I had you, I'd have everything."

It was over the top. It was sappy. Hell, it was downright cornpone. But, at that moment, nobody had said anything truer to Kate. And Ziggy meant it. He meant it all the way down.

They finished eating, still buzzing on the drug. They went back to the bar and made love in Ziggy's little nook, the floor hard and cold and Kate scratching up her knees, but the young man felt the barrier between him and his new love collapse. She was no longer acting, but losing herself in the release. They finally slept, waking as blue twilight tinted the back room.

Kate had to get home. There was only so much independence she had and would need to deal with Tony tonight. Ziggy was wrecked. The X had completely tapped his reserve of brain chemicals and he felt bolted to the floor. Zeppelin's was open for business and he cowered in his corner as the bartenders restocked. He fell asleep again at midnight, up in the early morning.

He had to get out on the road. Grand Coteau was far enough away to be an ordeal to get there and back in one day, but he needed to get the ring. He hoped Hildy would understand.

He got to the nunnery as mid-morning mass was letting out. He saw Hildy waddle out with all the other penguins while he sat on the hood of the Goat. She pulled away from the crowd, toward him.

"What are you doing?" She was lit up, ready to burst from her habit. "I thought I'd run away in the middle of the night. This is pretty bold."

"Yeah, you know me." He was straight up fronting, the silly grin plastered on his face as his insides fell southward. "The cavalry has come for the maiden in distress."

"I've been packed for a week. Come help me."

They went up to her room. In her closet were innocent looking suitcases. There was no indication this room was soon to be abandoned, or even that Hildy had spent the last twenty-three years living here.

"You really didn't want to be here, huh?"

"Kid, the day I checked in was the day I checked out. I thought of all this as Purgatory and I ain't staying anymore." She opened the top drawer and pulled out a jewelry box. "I believe this is yours."

He had dreamed about the ring for so long. It was still beautiful and now would finally pay off after years of personal escrow. He pulled it out of the box and slipped it onto his finger.

"Damn, it's so big."

"Football player's hand, babe. As big as you are, you still ain't no halfback."

"I think I'll keep it on for a while. Might be my only chance."

Ziggy grabbed two of three suitcases as Hildy stripped out of her habit, revealing her white t-shirt and jeans, the uniform of her past life. She folded up the black linen and grabbed her last case.

In the parking lot, Ziggy put the cases into the trunk. As Hildy exited, an older nun came running out after her. Ziggy sat in the driver's seat, watching the nun wagging her finger in Hildy's face. Hildy pivoted like she was going to walk away. When the nun grabbed her shoulder, Hildy swung back around, punching her in the jaw. The old woman crumpled in a heap of habit. Hildy laughed as she got in the car.

"God, did she deserve that!"

Ziggy pounded the accelerator and they were soon on the highway.

Hildy couldn't stop talking all the way back to New Orleans. She threw out all the neighborhoods they could live in, laid out plans for a new life. She pointed Ziggy in a thousand different directions, each idea more and more outlandish.

"I swear, Zig, I haven't felt like this in years. I feel like when I first met your dad and we could do anything the fuck we wanted. But now, it's even better. I don't have to worry about my dad approving or disapproving what I do. I have complete freedom. It's scary, but it's so fucking great."

Ziggy's balls withdrew into his crotch. He saw how unbound she was, how he was going to devastate her. But she was so much older than he. He had this whole new plan, a life path with a partner who wanted to seek out, not settle down. He was too young for all of this, all of her. He vowed to do right by her, for all the things she'd done, but he'd have to tell her the truth, quick as a bandage rip. As they crossed over the Bonne Carre Spillway, he started planning his speech.

They pulled up to Zeppelin's at about five o'clock. Ziggy waved her in as he stepped behind the bar.

"Don't worry, I know the owners."

"Dad bought Mimi's place?"

"Your guess is as good as mine. I was already gone. Beer?"

"Yeah. Dixie."

He popped open the brown bottle and poured himself a shot of Jack Daniels, covering it with ice and Coke. He slid her the beer, she sipping with relish.

"Yeah. That's the stuff."

"They didn't let you drink?"

"Sure they did. We ain't Baptists. But all the other birds drank wine. I just followed along." Ziggy shot his cocktail down in one swipe. "Hold that, tiger. You drink like we're running out of time."

Another shot, another spritz, and another down the hatch, he was ready to do what he had to. "We are. At least, you and me."

"The fuck you talking about?"

"When Kate gets here ..."

"Kate?"

"Mary Catherine."

"Jesus, twenty years up there and I just disappear, huh? Okay, when Kate gets here, what?"

"We're gonna move to Los Angeles. She's gonna make music and I'm gonna help her."

"Thought you couldn't go back."

"It's a big city. I'll stay on the down low while she does her thing."

"You're fucked in the head, Zig. You don't have any money and you don't have any job skills. You think she's gonna stick with nothing?"

"I got the ring. That'll hold us until she gets a deal. I figure we got a year."

"The ring. Lot of shit could've been avoided if that fucking dwarf had just walked away from the table."

"Don't worry about yourself. I'll give you as much as I can. You can start over."

"That's what you don't understand. I don't give a shit about myself. It may look like that, with our pillow talk and grand plans. But my life was never the question. It was your life that mattered."

"Well, I'm gonna make good on my life. I'll take care of you."

"Take care of me? Like my dad did? Like Norton did with Sealy?"

"I don't know about any of that. All I know is one person really took care of me and that was you. So, I'll help you start over and I'll move on with my life."

Hildy jumped off the barstool. She picked it up by the legs, smashing it twice against the bar, breaking it into six different pieces. She stood tall, holding one of the splintered legs. "You can't make good on a life of sin by making more sin."

"More of this bullshit."

Hildy dragged a hand across the bridge of her nose. "You don't see what has brought you here. You don't understand what God has planned for you. Yes, get rid of that ring. But only evil will come from the spoils."

"You're not doing a good job of making me stop."

"Then what do I have to do to put you on the righteous path?"

"Just get outta my way."

Ziggy walked toward the door, but Hildy pushed him back. He stumbled to the bar, both hands grabbing the rail. Hildy put a hand on his shoulder, but he swung angrily at her arm. It caught her square on the cheek, making a loud popping noise.

The instincts she had buried in her contemplative years returned in full. In one sharp blow to Ziggy's head, the stool leg caught him on the back of the neck. The quick crunch, a sound as innocuous as a knuckle crack, floored Ziggy.

In a matter of seconds, he was dead.

She fell to her knees, crying. One more mortal sin notched onto her, another mark of the beast to prove she wasn't fit to be part of this earth. She pulled the ring off of his finger and looked at it. She decided to rid the world of it.

She got the keys to the Goat. She started it up, pressing the pedal all the way down in park. It shook like a dragon ready for battle. She pulled her foot off the gas and threw it in gear. The sky was turning purple in the twilight when she pulled up in front of Tony's house, onto the lawn, pointing toward the door and leaning hard on the horn. Kate ran out.

"Ziggy, what the fuck?" She saw her half-sister. The normal smile was gone, Hildy's mouth locked in a grimace. "Hildy, where's Ziggy?"

"I killed him. Just like everyone that ever touched me. All dead."

Kate screamed at her sister, her voice cracking. "You did what? You bitch! I'll kill you."

Kate reached in to grab Hildy by the throat, but the sitting sister was too fast and too strong. A fist to Kate's chest crumpled her. Hildy leaned back on the horn as Kate struggled to get her breath.

And then he appeared in the doorway. He was double the size that Hildy remembered. He had to turn sideways to exit the front. His hair was still full, but it was leeched of color, a frighteningly pure white that also spread into his goatee. He was wearing a ratty terrycloth bathrobe and boxers. His face was cragged like poorly poured cement, but he turned and stared at his first born.

The good eye was clear and radiated hatred. He didn't wear the patch over the left socket, and the abyss, dark and mesmerizing, looked infinite.

Hildy looked at her father through the finger hole of the ring. She closed her left eye, mimicking Tony.

"We were all damned, Pops. It was written in the book long ago. I am just fulfilling the prophecy. Sin begets sin and the flames shall cleanse us." Hildy threw the car into drive.

Kate screamed with renewed breath as the car crashed through her father, through the door and through the house. Kate started to run toward the scene, but the car exploded before she could get too close. She was thrown back into the street, bangs and chin singed from the heat. She watched as the flames of her home illuminated the darkening sky, destroying the tender beauty of a twilit night.

Fat City Blues

ABOUT THE AUTHOR

Charlie Brown is a writer and filmmaker from New Orleans. He currently lives in Los Angeles, where he recently received his Masters in Professional Writing from the University of Southern California and also runs Lucky Mojo Press and Mojotooth Productions. He has made two feature films: "Angels Die Slowly" and "Never A Dull Moment: 20 Years of the Rebirth Brass Band." His fiction has appeared in Oddville Press, Writing Disorder, Jersey Devil Press, The Menacing Hedge, Aethlon, and what?? Magazine. He also edited and published the "Dirty Magick" anthologies.

http://www.charliebrownwriter.com
http://www.mojotoothproductions.com
http://www.luckymojopress.com

Also available from Lucky Mojo Press on Amazon.com:

www.ingramcontent.com/pod-product-compliance
Lightning Source LLC
Chambersburg PA
CBHW020633130626
46552CB00003B/1202